THE BIG BRAND

"The short story is a classic form for Western fiction. When I was a boy growing up on a West Texas ranch in the 1930s, eagerly reading everything I could find about the West in general and Texas in particular, it seemed to be the dominant form in the weekly and monthly magazines, over even the novel.

"The beauty of these stories to me, besides their ability to transport me to a long-ago time of romance and adventure, was that I could read one in twenty or thirty minutes stolen between daily chores or school lessons, or just before being marched off to an ice-cold bed on a winter's evening.

"It helped take the edge off of the monotony to be able to imagine ourselves driving a herd to the railroad in Dodge City or to be searching the brushy draws for desperate rustlers instead of for screwworm-infested calves we had to doctor with a black syrupy mixture that smelled like death and wouldn't scrub off of our hands."

—From the Introduction

Other books by Elmer Kelton

THE BIG BRAND

Elmer Kelton

BANTAM BOOKS
TORONTO • NEW YORK • LONDON • SYDNEY • AUCKLAND

THE BIG BRAND

A Bantam Book/December 1986

The stories in this volume first appeared in the following
publications in slightly different form:

"Fighting for the Brand," Texas Rangers magazine, New
York, September 1956.

"Yellow Devil," Ranch Romances magazine, New York, April
25, 1952.

"Jailbreak," Western Short Stories, New York, September
1956.

"That 7X Bull," from Western Roundup, WWA Anthology,
Macmillan, New York, 1961.

"Lonesome Ride to Pecos," Ranch Romances, New York, April
29, 1949.

"Coward," Ranch Romances, New York, January 1, 1954.

"Horse Well," Ranch Romances, New York, February 1,
1952.

"Duster," Farm Journal, Philadelphia, April 1956.

"The Debt of Hardy Buckelew," from Frontiers West, WWA
Anthology, Doubleday & Co., New York, 1959.

"Relics," Far West magazine, Costa Mesa, California, No-
vember 1978.

"Uncle Jeff and the Gunfighter," from The Pick of the Roundup,
WWA Anthology, Ace Books, New York, 1962.

"O'Malley's Wife," Ranch Romances, New York, March 22,
1957.

ISBN 0-553-26147-9

Published simultaneously in the United States and Canada

Bantam Books are published by Bantam Books, Inc. Its trademark, consisting of the words "Bantam Books" and the por-
trayal of a rooster, is Registered in U.S. Patent and Trademark
Office and in other countries. Marca Registrada. Bantam
Books, Inc., 666 Fifth Avenue, New York, New York 10103.

PRINTED IN THE UNITED STATES OF AMERICA

O   0 9 8 7 6 5 4 3 2 1

Contents

Introduction

The short story is a classic form for Western fiction. When I was a boy growing up on a West Texas ranch in the 1930s, eagerly reading everything I could find about the West in general and Texas in particular, it seemed to be the dominant form, over even the novel. Our Crane, Texas, drugstores offered big stacks of weekly and monthly magazines devoted entirely to the Western. Each issue typically would contain one or two novelettes and perhaps half a dozen short stories featuring many of the leading names in the Western field. In addition, prestigious "slick" magazines such as the *Saturday Evening Post* sometimes offered Western short stories by honored writers, including Ernest Haycox, Luke Short, and S. Omar Barker.

The beauty of these stories to me, besides their ability to transport me to a long-ago time of romance and adventure, was that I could read one in twenty or thirty minutes stolen between daily chores or school lessons, or just before being marched off to an ice-cold bed on a winter's evening. The pleasant afterglow would sustain me through the mundane necessity of chopping wood, feeding horses, or milking the cow, or would send me contentedly off to sleep.

When we were not in school, we Kelton boys spent a lot of time on horseback, working cattle alongside the grown cowboys and my father, the ranch foreman. The work was often hard and gritty, and not nearly so glamorous as it seemed in the movies or in the stories I read. It helped take the edge off of the monotony to be able to imagine ourselves driving a herd to the railroad in Dodge City, or to be searching the brushy draws for desperate rustlers instead of for screwworm-infested calves we had to doctor with a black syrupy mixture that smelled like death and wouldn't scrub off of our hands.

My mother, a former schoolteacher, had read stories to me when I was small, and taught me to read for myself when I was five years old. When I started to school at age seven, I was given a test and put in the third grade. That made me the runt in all my classes, too small to hold my own in football with the "big" boys or to compete successfully with them in other athletics. My refuge was reading. I read everything that came to hand, no matter what its subject matter. But I always kept coming back to material about the West. Growing up far out in the country, in an environment of cowboys, cattle, and horses, I never wearied of the subject, even though as a cowboy I was hopelessly inept, a constant source of despair for my father.

One of my great-grandfathers had come out to West Texas from the piney woods in the 1870s, bringing a covered wagon and a string of horses. Another great-grandfather had run cattle in the Indian Territory. My father's father had to go to work at age twelve, punching cattle and breaking horses and mules to help support his mother and younger brothers and sisters after his own father had died too young on a Callahan County homestead.

Some of the older men who were friends of my father and grandfather had been young cowboys in the open-range and trail-driving days. The first funeral I can remember attending was of a neighbor, an elderly ranchman said to have hunted buffalo in his youth. As a boy I sat slack-jawed, listening to stories by or about these men. Living the isolated lives that they did, the cowboys I knew in my boyhood tended to be gregarious when the opportunity arose. Telling stories, and listening to them, was one of their favorite pastimes, and as a group they tended to be good oral storytellers. My father, though he never wrote anything longer than a letter, was one of the best storytellers I ever knew when he was sitting around a campfire at the chuckwagon or on the porch of the bunkhouse.

Cowboys themselves loved to read Western stories, vicariously experiencing through fiction the excitement and romance that were supposed to be part and parcel of the West but often seemed missing from their own lives. Most bunkhouses in those days had several Western pulp magazines lying around, and a slightly older cousin of mine, a good cowboy himself, introduced me to the grand pleasures of Zane Grey.

Today's cowboys no longer have access to the pulp magazines of that time, but cowboys are among the most eager followers of Louis L'Amour and other popular Western writers.

All this early love of story stuck to me like that unscrubbable screwworm killer, and I knew even as a boy that I wanted to write stories of my own. I started with short, wildly-imaginative yarns scribbled in school tablets and composition books, hidden away lest someone discover my secret. Writing stories seemed less manly and respectable than playing football, for which I was too small, or roping calves, which my loops always missed.

At age sixteen I entered the University of Texas, studying toward a degree in journalism, which I thought was my most likely avenue for working into a writing career. After returning from infantry service in World War II and resuming my interrupted work at the university, I began writing with a serious intention of publishing. As did most other aspiring young writers of the time, I turned toward my old love, the short story. I studied books on writing and spent hours dissecting stories by writers I liked, trying to learn how and why they did as they did. I wrote stories and mailed them to magazines, and at times they seemed to beat me home from the post office. After more than a year of trying and receiving rejections on twenty or thirty stories, I finally managed to sell one to the venerable *Ranch Romances*, one of the leaders in the pulp field. It was almost another year before I sold my second. But after that, sales came with increasing regularity, and I felt proud to see my name appear on title pages along with those of writers whose work I had admired and studied for years. They never knew how much help they had given me.

Short stories in general, not just Western short stories, seem to have become an endangered species in recent times. Most fiction magazines that featured them have disappeared from the scene, and relatively few new short stories find a home today. This is regrettable, for some of the finest literature in the English language is to be found in the short-story form. Many of the most honored novelists learned the rudiments of their art and craft while writing short stories. The short story gave generations of aspiring young writers the opportunity to earn while they learned. The beginning writer today must start with the novel, a bit like pushing him or her off of an ocean liner with a command to learn how to swim.

Though I have concentrated on the novel for most of the last thirty years, I still welcome the occasional opportunity to do a short story. Its brevity makes it look deceptively easy in comparison to the far longer novel form, but it presents challenges of its own that can be formidable. Where the novel affords the writer room to expand and explore and develop story and character with some leisure, the short story requires rapid establishment of the scene, the situation, and the people involved. It demands an economy of words and a merciless pruning of the dispensable. Just as the stopwatch ticks mercilessly for the competing athlete as he races toward the finish line, the word count ticks in the writer's mind as he tries to get a story told solidly and entertainingly within the tight limitations of the form.

The short stories in this collection are selected from some fifty or so that I published in the early years of my writing career and have continued to publish at intervals, even after beginning to devote most of my writing time to novels of Texas and the West. All are set in my native Texas, of which I write most because I know it best. They offer a cross section of types. Some are traditional action stories of bad men and peace officers and gunfights. Some have no guns at all, but tell of Western people as I have known them, standing up to challenges of nature or circumstances with only their wits, their determination, and their strong sense of honor, duty, and right.

The first story, "Fighting for the Brand," is built around one of the unwritten but honored rules of the cowboy—that he remain faithful to an outfit so long as he worked for it, no matter what the cost. In cowboy parlance, it was stated, "Never cuss the man who pays you." If the cowboy could not accept that, his only honorable alternative was to ask for his time and leave. The story is set in the Texas Panhandle, where some of the largest ranches were put together in the 1870s and 1880s. Ranches occasionally feuded with one another. One of the biggest and deadliest gunfights in wild old Tascosa grew out of rivalry between cowboys of two large plains ranches.

"Yellow Devil" tells of a young man's struggle against nature, in this case a horse-killing mountain lion, and his feeling of obligation to repay a debt not entirely his own, even against the will of the man to whom he owed it. This story is set in the beautifully rugged Big Bend area of far West Texas, a region not often treated in fiction.

"That 7X Bull" takes place along the caprock where the uplifted Llano Estacado breaks away toward the rolling plains. It tells of a proud and scrappy old cowhand, regarded as having outlived his time, and his reluctant quest to destroy an aging range bull that is another defiant relic of a bygone day. As a sidelight I would add that each cowboy generation for a hundred years seems to have considered itself the last of the breed. The cowboy today keeps on keeping on, adjusting to the times and technology, and surviving.

"Jailbreak" is a traditional action story of a man whose long search brings him face to face with his quarry almost too late, and forces him to a hard choice that severely challenges his strict code of ethics.

"Lonesome Ride to Pecos" is set in the dry Pecos River country of West Texas, where economic survival has always been a challenge. It tells of a lawman who cannot allow his regret for what he has had to do prevent him from taking the necessary second step and doing what he knows he will regret even more.

"Coward" happens during the fence wars of Central Texas in the early 1880s, a struggle between the free-range men and those who sought to enclose their lands with barbed wire. In history, some of the bitterest fights were in Brown and Coleman counties. Though the incident did not find a place in my story, the fence cutters in Brown County burned the courthouse to destroy the official records and hamper their prosecution. Fence troubles led finally to a Texas state law passed as an emergency measure, making it illegal to carry a set of wire pinchers on a saddle. That century-old law is still on the books, or was the last time I checked. As a youngster helping fix fence, I broke it many times.

"Horse Well" is a real place on the McElroy Ranch in Crane County, the place where I grew up, though the story is a figment of an active imagination. When I was a boy we used to camp the chuckwagon near the old well when we were working cattle on that part of the ranch. Old-timers told a legend about horse thieves who had murdered a cowboy some miles to the east and were overtaken and killed when they stopped to water their horses. As the story went, their bodies were tossed into the hand-dug well. When I was a boy, that haunted well had a morbid fascination for me. In later years I learned that the first part of the story was indeed true, and I came upon the cowboy's grave several times in the ranch's big south pasture. But the part about retribution at Horse Well was without foundation. The principal culprit was tried, convicted, and legally hanged, miles away. The groans I heard coming from the old well were simply the sucker rod rubbing against the pipe deep in the hole, like my father tried to tell me in the first place.

"The Debt of Hardy Buckelew" is set on the early trail drives, of which stories used to send chills up my back when I was a boy, listening to campfire talk. The longest cattle drive I ever made was three days to the shipping pens at

Odessa from the McElroy Ranch, but it was enough to make those old stories alive and real for me, then and now. The biggest challenge the trail drivers had to contend with were natural—the long dry stretches, the stampedes, the storms, and the rivers that had to be crossed. There was no way to face them except head-on, and this the old-timers did. If Texans today still have a reputation for stubbornness, their forebears earned it honestly, doing what had to be done in defiance of whatever odds might arise.

"Relics," set in the Texas lower plains country near the New Mexico line, is a story of an old chuckwagon cook who fights with the only weapon at his command and exacts a terrible vengeance. As a boy growing up, I knew several wagon cooks, a couple of them very well, and either might have done what the cook in the story does, given the circumstances. It was drilled into me from as far back as I can remember that around the wagon the cook was the lord and master, and woe to the horse jingler or cowhand who rode too close to his fire and stirred dust into his cooking, who failed to clean his own plate and drop it into the wreck pan, or who failed to roll up his own bed and leave it near the wagon for easy loading.

"O'Malley's Wife" centers on sheep, a subject not widely addressed in Western stories except in negative terms. Most often the sheepman has been portrayed either as a willful despoiler of the range or as a meek, almost cowardly type no braver than the animals in his charge. It is true that there was occasional warfare between sheepman and cattleman in the Old West, but this grew mostly out of the cattleman's misunderstanding of the effect sheep had on the grass. The truth—and Texas cattlemen eventually learned it—was that sheep properly handled could actually improve a range. They spoiled it only if grossly overstocked. Cattle would do the same under those circumstances. The story's plot is loosely based upon an actual incident on the Middle Concho River west of San Angelo, Texas, and hinges on the fact that under Texas law the state and the public own the riverbeds up to the outer bank, no matter who owns the land on either side.

"Uncle Jeff and the Gunfighter" is set in the Pecos River country in the turn-of-the-century days of Texas's four-section homesteaders, when the state bet a piece of dry land against three years of a settler's life that he could not stay. In an actual case, a rancher who had been using state land near the Pecos River hired a regionally notorious gunfighter named Jim Miller to scare four-sectioners out of the country. Miller did frighten some, but others managed to give him a bigger scare than he gave, and he fled the country, only to run afoul of an Oklahoma lynch mob not long afterward. My story was suggested by that situation, and the classic open-ended question, "What if?"

"Duster" is a modern-times story, more or less. It was based on the same long 1950s drouth as my novel, "The Time It Never Rained." In a sense that novel was an outgrowth of this story. Drouth has long been the most implacable foe of the ranching industry in the West because there are so few things a ranchman can do to fight it except, in the words of President Lyndon Johnson, "hunker down like a jackrabbit in a hailstorm" and endure. The drouth in this story lasted seven years. That was a lot of endurance.

ELMER KELTON
San Angelo, Texas
1986

THE BIG
BRAND

Fighting for the Brand

You hear a lot of talk nowadays about loyalty and what it means. Old-time cowboys knew what it meant. The loyalty they had to the brand they worked for has seldom been equaled, before or since. Sometimes they loved the outfit; sometimes they didn't. But as long as they rode its horses and ate its grub and drew its pay, they were loyal. Even when that meant risking their lives for it. Even when it meant taking up a gun against a friend.

Up in the Texas Panhandle, old-timers still talk about the day Shag Fristo and Curly Jim came riding into Dry Fork, pockets empty and the seats of their pants shiny and thin from rubbing a saddle so long.

They were cousins, but it didn't show.

Curly was the short one, his shoulders as thick and broad as an ax handle is long. And he was always grinning, even the few times he ever got mad. The boys said he slept grinning. Riding into Dry Fork, he was singing to himself. Not pretty, but loud enough that he couldn't hear his stomach growling at him.

Shag Fristo was the one folks always looked back at a second time. He was uncommonly tall, his shoulders a little slumped, the way those old cowboys often got. His hands were as big as a saddle blanket. His rusty red hair bristled out over his ears, the reason people called him Shag. He was scowling that day because he was thirsty and hungry. That always made him restless, and restlessness usually put him in a frame of mind for a fight. He hadn't had a fight for the better part of a month.

1

That fight had had far-reaching implications, however, and was the reason Shag and Curly Jim were riding the chuckline, looking for work. They'd been playing a peaceful game of poker down in the Pecos country when the house man had decided he didn't like the cut of Shag's clothes, or maybe the lack of cut of his hair, and Shag had decided he didn't like the cut of the deck. The disagreement had wound up with the saloonkeeper looking for somebody to help him build the saloon back, and the sheriff looking for Shag.

Shag's scowl deepened as he reined his sorrel horse toward the twin set of wagon ruts that passed for a street in Dry Fork. There were two rows of sunbaked adobes, with a few new lumber houses sitting up on blocks so high off the ground they made Shag think of a barefooted fat woman hoisting her skirts to wade a puddle of water.

Shag pulled out a lonesome-looking silver dollar. "Last steer from a mighty herd," he said. "Do we eat it or drink it?"

"Flip it," said Curly.

"Heads for whisky, tails for beef." Shag flipped it, caught it in his hand and slapped it down on his thick red wrist so hard the dust flew. He swore under his breath. Tails.

In the little box-and-strip eating place they hungrily inspected the quarter of good red beef hanging up there, then laid their silver dollar on the counter and took chili.

Cornering the last spoonful, Curly asked the slump-shouldered cook, "You know any outfit that needs a couple of good hands? Shag here can ride and rope anything that's got hair on it, and I'm better than he is."

Just a chuckwagon cook moved to town, the cafe man nodded his bald head. "Matter of fact, I do. Old Man Jesse Wheat out at the Flying W was in this mornin', lookin' for a cowboy."

Curly stood up, wiping the chili from his chin. "Let's go, Shag."

The cook held up his dough-crusted hand. "Just a minute there. I said *a* cowboy. When Jesse Wheat says *one*, he means one. Kind of set in his ways, he is."

2

THE BIG BRAND

Thoughtfully Curly and Shag eyed each other. Curly looked at the few cents change and said with regret, "We better do it, cousin. Maybe it won't be for long."

Shag picked up a coin and flipped it.

"Heads I take it, tails you do." It was tails again.

So Curly rode out for the Flying W, but not before he had dug deep into his war bag and pulled out his most prized possession, a pair of silver-mounted spurs. He had won them roping steers against another roper of some reputation down in South Texas. He had never once contaminated them with horse sweat.

"If you don't find you a job pretty quick," he told Shag, "you're liable to need these. Somebody ought to pay a right smart for them."

So it was that Shag Fristo and Curly Jim got tallied out to different brands. It was the first time in years the cousins had been more than rock-chunking distance apart.

Shag took the change from the dollar and went down to the wagon yard. A friendly little game of poker got started on a saddle blanket. By suppertime Shag had won enough to buy chili for several days, along with prairie hay for his sorrel horse.

Next day he was sitting in the shade of the livery barn, thinking of buying that saddle blanket and a deck of cards and setting up in business for himself. A buckboard came rattling into town, its dust winding down past the wagon yard and drifting up to the doctor's house.

Two men followed it on horseback. One of them shot a quick, hard glance at Shag. He was a little old wrinkled-up man with bristly gray whiskers as stiff as barbed wire and eyes that looked like the business ends of two .45 cartridges.

"That there's Skinner Hamilton," the hostler informed Shag, pointing the stem of a pipe that would knock down a grown dog. "Owns the Rafter H, and is as ornery as a wildcat with the hives. Him and Old Man Jesse Wheat, they're like a couple of fightin' roosters. Been feudin' so long they probably don't neither one of them remember what started it."

3

"Wheat?" Shag frowned. That was the man Curly Jim had gone to work for.

The hostler nodded. "They're both old bachelors. Stands to reason a woman caused the bust-up. And here of late it's broke out kind of mean. Been a little old squatter outfit between their ranches for years. This squatter, he had the best hole of water in fifty miles of here. A little while back he quit. Left the country.

"Some folks say Jesse and Skinner squeezed him out. I reckon that's more idle talk than solid information, but anyhow the minute the squatter's wagon and his cattle went out of sight over the hill, them two had their cowpunchers pushin' cattle in behind them. They been playin' tug-of-war ever since. Jesse's men hold the water a few days and don't let nothin' drink there but Flying W cattle. Then Skinner's bunch shows up and runs them off, and they chase out everything but Rafter H stuff.

"Folks call it the banty rooster feud. It'd be comical if they wasn't gettin' so serious. Liable to be a killin' out there yet, you watch what I tell you."

About then the two men Shag had won the money from came back with a fresh stake. In considerably less time than it had taken him to win it, he lost the whole wad. So Skinner Hamilton struck him at the right moment.

The old man stood there and looked Shag up and down like he was a horse or a plow mule. "Man tells me you're lookin' for work."

Shag nodded. The old man looked at him harder, as if about to chew him up and spit him out. "You're not one of them newfangled cowboys that wants to quit soon's it's dark and expects to laze around all day Sunday, are you?"

Shag solemnly assured him he worked twenty-six hours a day, forty days a month.

The old man chewed his tobacco and kept looking him up and down. "One more thing, then." He motioned Shag into the livery barn and pointed at a stack of hundred-pound grain bags. "See how hard you can hit that top sack."

Shag put his shoulder into it and hit the sack so hard

4

it tumbled off. The stitching broke, spilling grain on the dirt floor.

Skinner's whiskered jaw worked the tobacco faster. "You'll do." He turned to a man who had ridden in with him, a medium-tall cowboy with a cut and bruised face and one eye a shade blue. "This here's my foreman, Peeler Milholland."

Shag shook Milholland's hand. "Pleased to meet you."

Milholland just nodded. Shag looked into his eye—the one that wasn't swollen shut—and thought he could see sympathy there. Or perhaps it was just pain.

At the ranch that night, Shag studied the faces of the cowboys over his plate of beef and frijoles. Every man looked as if he had stumbled and fallen into a meat grinder—black eyes, skinned noses, blue-bruised cheekbones.

After supper Skinner Hamilton called him out beneath the cool branches of a huge old cottonwood tree. The old man tried to sit down on his heels with Shag's easy grace. Halfway down he caught himself and straightened up, swearing, his gnarled old hand pushing against his hip to get the kink out.

"Reckon you heard in town about that connivin' old cow thief they call Jesse Wheat?"

"A little bit," Shag admitted.

"You know he's tryin' to take away a waterhole that's mine by rights? Tryin' to starve my poor old cows to death, rob me of fifty years' rightful gatherin'?"

Shag said he'd heard a little mention of it.

Skinner's wizened face clouded up. "He's as mean as a rattlesnake. Cunnin' as a fox. Greedy as an old boar."

With what little tact he had, Shag said, "Man told me you-all used to be friends, a long time ago."

Skinner violently shook his gray head. "I was too young to know any better." A glow came into the lead-gray eyes. "You know what the old chickensnake done last night? I had five men down at the waterhole, mindin' their own business, just seein' to it that my cows got all they wanted to drink. That old warthog come a-chargin' in with thirty gunslingers—twenty, anyway—and beat one of my boys up so bad I had to haul him to town."

Skinner pointed a crooked forefinger at Shag. "But you're a man that can put him in his place. Use them fists a little bit, and old Jesse won't dare to come back, ever."

From what Shag had heard, old Jesse *would* come back. In fact, it'd probably tickle him to death to try.

But Shag didn't say so. Especially since he hadn't drawn any pay yet.

The cowboys groaned when Peeler Milholland passed on Skinner's orders to load their guns and saddle their broncs. "Even whisky never was as habit formin' as this," one limping cowpuncher complained.

But not one of them failed to go along, or even hesitated more than long enough to stretch his sore limbs. They rode at a stiff trot, not joshing each other or spinning windies to pass away the miles the way cowboys usually do. Weariness lay heavily on every man's shoulders, but a dogged persistence kept them going. As for Shag, the prospect of a little fight didn't bother him. His fist was itching a little.

He grinned as a thought struck him. What if Curly Jim was there? It would be a laugh if Shag got to boot him in the britches. It would be something Shag could hooraw him about someday when they were working together again.

Shag sensed the temper of the cowboys changing as they approached the waterhole. Any resentment, any reluctance seemed to fade. Now, no matter what, they were Rafter H men, and there was pride in that fact.

Skinner Hamilton raised his knotty fist and said, "We'll give old Jesse somethin' to rattle what teeth he's got left! We'll show him what's the top outfit in this here country."

It was like a shot of whisky starting a man's blood to pumping again.

Times, maybe, these punchers got mad enough at Skinner Hamilton to spit in his bloodshot eye. But now they were with him all the way.

Not far from the waterhole they reined up for a hasty war parley, hardly able to see each other in the dim light of the quarter moon.

"They're bound to have a guard out," Milholland said.

"Well, now," Shag volunteered, "I'm the new man around here. How about me doin' the missionary work?"

He was elected. He hung his jingling spurs over the saddle horn so as not to disturb any Flying W men who might have retired early and needed their rest. He handed the reins to somebody and set out afoot.

The waterhole was bright silver under the thin wood shaving of a moon. Cattle were bedded down not far from its banks. Up at the head of it, Shag had been told, a little spring bubbled water enough to keep the hole full but not enough to start a running stream.

Presently he spotted the guard. A match flared, and a freshly rolled cigarette glowed. Shag rubbed his knuckles.

He moved around behind the man and tapped him on the shoulder. When the guard looked back, there was a quick, solid thud and the cigarette went sailing. Shag rubbed his smarting knuckles again. The skin was torn, maybe bleeding a little.

He hadn't felt so good in weeks.

He looked down at the groggy man, and his mouth dropped open. It was all he could do to keep from laughing out loud.

Curly Jim would never hear the last of this.

Still laughing inside, Shag walked on up to the campfire. Only five men here. He squalled like a panther and headed for the first man who jumped up.

By the time the rest of the Rafter H got there, they didn't have much to do.

When Skinner Hamilton strutted around later, crowing about what "we" had done, something went sour in Shag's stomach. Damned old pelican hadn't bruised a knuckle.

And suddenly Shag wondered if the old rancher ever had. He was mighty good at exercising his jaw. But had he ever done a lick of real fighting himself against this Jesse Wheat he hated so all-fired much?

Skinner delegated Shag and four others to stay on and let the Rafter H cattle come up to water. He suggested that they kind of drift the Flying W stock away a little piece, say ten or fifteen miles.

Only a pile of charred poles showed where the squatter's shack had been. It had fallen victim in the first tussle over this waterhole. Now a well-stocked chuckbox was set up in the open shade of the cottonwoods. Scattered about on the ground was the bedding the Flying W's had left in their obliging retreat. Shag wondered how often the chuckbox and the bedding had already changed hands.

It came close to changing hands that afternoon. Out pushing away Wheat's cattle, Shag saw the Flying W's coming. He and the other Hamilton cowhands got back to the waterhole first. They were sitting there diligently rubbing their guns to a high polish when the eight riders came up.

Curly Jim wasn't with them, Shag noted with amusement. Probably soaking his aching jaw in a wet cloth somewhere.

Shag had never seen Jesse Wheat, but he knew him now on sight. Wheat was about the same cut of man as Skinner Hamilton, two years older than the Canadian River, and wrinkled up like a peach seed. His beard was a shade shorter but just as gray as Skinner's and just as scraggly. He had the same kind of piercing eyes, and the same fierce pride was shining in them.

Old Man Wheat frowned at the guns in the punchers' hands. "You fellers don't need them things. We didn't come here to fight. We just come to ask you to move along peaceable."

The old man had more gall than a bull yearling. Shag stood up to his full six-feet-five and laughed in Jesse Wheat's face.

The rancher's eyes snapped. "You're the one," he accused. "You're the one hurt my poor boys last night." Then the eyes stopped snapping. The same calculating look came into them that had been in Skinner's when Shag had knocked the grain bag down with his fist.

"You know, cowboy," he said confidentially, "that's a sorry greasy-sack outfit you're a-runnin' with. You'll die ragged and in disgrace, workin' for an old turkey buzzard like Skinner Hamilton. Why don't you come on and ride for me?"

Shag shook his head. "Skinner Hamilton's buyin' my grub and payin' my wages. I reckon I'll stay."

Wheat shrugged. "Your funeral, then. All right, boys. Take 'em!"

The Flying W's jumped down and came swarming. In about two minutes it was over with, and Shag had *two* sets of skinned knuckles.

Old Man Jesse Wheat sat in his saddle, blinking in disbelief at his cowboys piled up like cordwood.

"Now you've *really* split your britches," he raged, when his Adam's apple quit bobbing. "The Flyin' W will cut you down to size. You watch."

Helping Wheat's battered cowboys back into their saddles, Shag got the notion they weren't quite so enthusiastic.

But they'd try again. That was the cowboy way. They'd try as often as Jesse Wheat said to, as long as they stayed on his payroll. They might finally draw their pay and leave, but they'd never let up as long as they worked for him.

They didn't let up. They came again that night, and the next night. They came with guns and tried to scare off the Rafter H men by sending bullets whining high over their heads. But Shag Fristo stood solid as a rock wall and aimed his gun a little lower.

Skinner Hamilton listened to the telling of it, a malevolent grin splitting his whiskery face. "Old Jesse'll bust a blood vessel," he said gleefully.

But Peeler Milholland, the foreman, was less than gleeful. "First time it's ever come to shootin'. Anything can happen now."

Shag tried to ease him. "Aw, it wasn't much. Nobody got shot at. Just a few cartridges got burnt up."

"But what about the next time?" Peeler demanded, flicking a quick, half-angry look at old Skinner dancing around as if he had just raked in the whole pot from a high-stakes table. "Somebody's liable to get killed, and there ain't enough water in Texas to be worth that."

If Skinner Hamilton heard him, he showed no sign of it.

* * *

The next time was not long in coming. It was that night. There was little warning, just all of a sudden a clatter of hoofs and the yells of the Flying W men sweeping down like demons after a three-day drunk. Scattered all around the waterhole, Skinner Hamilton's cattle jumped to their feet and broke into a run. The Flying W's fired their guns into the air.

The Rafter H horses stampeded in terror, all but one hobbled in camp. He reared and threshed and threw himself to the ground, fighting the rawhide thongs that bound his forefeet.

Nothing is more useless than a cowboy left afoot. Shag grabbed a rope and ran after the threshing horse as it struggled to its feet and tried to run away in an awkward three-legged gait. He swung the loop, made his catch, and whipped the end of the rope around his hip, digging his high heels into the ground. The panicked horse turned back, fighting the rope.

Then, from out of the darkness, a rider bore down on him, firing into the air, trying to make the horse break away.

In a flush of fury, Shag pulled out his own pistol and aimed over the cowboy's head, hoping to booger him away. He fired once . . . twice. Then, as he squeezed the trigger again, the horse made a hard lunge. The gun jerked down.

The thud of the bullet was thunder loud to Shag. The man cried out and tumbled from his saddle.

Cold fear hit Shag a belly blow. He ran to the fallen rider. "Lord of mercy, man," he cried, "I didn't mean—"

He turned the man over, and all the strength dropped out of him. Curly Jim!

Eyes burning, Shag felt for the wound and found it, low in the shoulder. He pulled his hand away, warm and sticky.

"Curly . . ." His voice broke. "I swear to God, I wouldn't of shot you for the world."

The shooting and yelling had stopped. Friend and foe,

10

they all gathered around and stood, dull from shock, looking at Shag Fristo and Curly Jim.

"We got to get him to town," Shag said.

He and a Flying W man stanched the bleeding and wrapped the wound. There was no wagon, so they caught Curly's horse and put him back on it. Shag threw his own rig on the horse with which he had been struggling. With the Flying W man to help him, he headed for town, holding Curly in the saddle.

One of the Rafter H cowboys ran to catch up with him "Old Skinner ain't goin' to like this. What can I tell him?"

Shag's voice ripped like barbed wire. "Tell him to go to hell!"

The doctor never was going to get through in there, it seemed like. Shag had drunk so much coffee his stomach sloshed when he moved. But he was boiling up another pot of it, his red-webbed eyes on the door behind which the doctor worked. The Flying W man sat patiently watching him. He knew about the kinship between Shag and Curly Jim.

He suggested, "Why don't you set down a spell and get some shut-eye? I'll wake you up when the doc comes out."

Shag walked wearily to the window and looked out into the new day. This was all his fault. Remorse clung to him, heavy as lead.

"I won't be able to sleep till I know if Curly's goin' to make it." He lowered his red head. "If he don't . . ." He did not speak the thought aloud, but if Curly died, Shag was liable to kill a couple of iron-headed old ranchers.

The cowboy nodded sympathetically and joined Shag at looking out the window. "I'm scared, Shag," he confessed. "This business has come to a head, I'm thinkin'. Liable to be a hell of a fight out at that waterhole today."

Shag's face was hard and grim. He doubled his big fists. Hadn't those stiff-necked old warhorses had enough?

The door hinges creaked, and the doctor stepped in.

11

He was not exactly smiling, but his eyes bespoke confidence. "Your friend is made out of rawhide and barbed wire. He'll make it."

On his way back to the waterhole, Shag rode hard and steadily, irritably touching spurs to his horse any time the animal lagged or pulled to one side or the other. Shag's eyes were bloodred from loss of sleep, and they burned as if they had sand in them. He hadn't eaten any breakfast, so hunger was working on him. All in all, he was in no humor for church.

Mostly his mind was on Curly Jim. Curly had every right never to speak to him again. But the first thing Curly had done when he had opened his eyes was to grin and call him a name that could only be considered profane.

That was more than being kin. That was friendship.

Even before Shag got to the waterhole he could see that the Flying W puncher had been right. There, on the west, the whole Flying W was lined up on either side of Old Jesse Wheat. On the east, every man from the Rafter H even to the cook was siding old Skinner Hamilton. There was enough artillery in the outfit to reopen the Civil War.

Shag noted with a scowl that only two men in the whole bunch were not packing iron—Skinner Hamilton and Jesse Wheat.

The two wrinkled old ranchers hunched on their horses, hurling threats and barbed language in each other's direction. Skinner cut his angry eyes at Shag. "Where the hell you been?"

Shag growled some kind of answer.

"High time you got back!" Skinner grumbled. "We're fixin' to have us a showdown here, for once and for all. We need every gun we got."

Something was simmering inside of Shag like chili on a hot stove. He pointed his red-stubbled chin at Skinner's hip. "I don't see yours."

Skinner's face flamed. He wasn't used to being spoken to this way. Not by anybody but Jesse Wheat.

"I got a good mind to fire you, Fristo."

"You ain't *got* any mind, and you can't fire me. I done

quit." He reached down and came up with his pistol. He motioned at Skinner. "Git down."

Skinner's mouth dropped open. "You've gone crazy, that's what."

"Probably. But I said git down. And you too, Jesse Wheat."

Dumbfounded, the two oldsters looked to their men for help. Shag made a sweeping motion with the gun. "All you fellers move around here in front of me, to where I can see you. First man reaches for a gun is apt to get his toes shot off."

Nobody wanted to get burned, so everybody stood off and looked at him. He went on, "These two old buzzards been wantin' a showdown, and I think it's time they had one. It ought to've been done twenty or thirty years ago." He turned to Hamilton and Wheat. "This time you two are goin' to fight it out yourselves instead of lettin' your cowpunchers beat their brains out for you. Hit him, Skinner!"

The old man hesitated. Shag pulled back the hammer. It clicked loudly enough to be heard across the county line.

Skinner swung his fist weakly and gave Wheat a tap.

"Harder! Make it a good one."

The second one made both men grunt.

"That's more like it. Now, Wheat, you hit him back."

Wheat did.

"Go on and fight now, both of you. Get it out of your damned systems for once and for all."

Looking apprehensively at Shag, the two ranchers went at each other like two tired old bulls, half the time swinging so wildly they didn't even connect. When it looked as though they might stop, Shag motioned with the gun again.

"Keep it up. You ain't half started yet."

So they fought and wrestled, rolling over and over in the dirt, losing their hats, tearing buttons from their shirts. Neither could hit hard enough to break the shell on an egg. Shag stood over them menacingly. Each time it looked as though they might give up, he gently nuzzled one or the other in the ribs with the barrel of the pistol.

Their fierce dignity gone, the two old ranchers were

an almost ludicrous sight. One by one, the cowboys began to grin.

It went on and on until finally both men tottered in the mud at the edge of the waterhole, dirty and disheveled, their clothes hanging, sweat streaking the dust on their faces. Skinner gave Wheat one final tap and fell on his face in the water. Wheat sat down with a muddy splash.

Skinner rolled over and wiped the water from his face, leaving a broad track of mud. Both men were heaving for breath. For a long time they sat in the water and stared at each other. They were a sorry-looking spectacle, the both of them. They looked as if they knew it.

Jesse Wheat said finally, "Skinner, you look like hell."

Skinner rubbed another smear of mud across his face. "You ain't no mornin' glory yourself."

Shag Fristo towered over the two men, his lips tight against his teeth. "Now then," he said brittlely, "there's water enough here for both of you, and you're goin' to share it. If ever I hear of you two old terrapins raisin' hell with each other again, I'll come back and rub them two gray heads together till by Judas you can smell the hair burn!"

Stiffly he walked back to his horse.

Jesse Wheat followed him with his eyes. "Skinner," he said, "maybe you'd let a man like that get away, but I'll be dogged if I will. If you ain't takin' him back to your ranch, I'm takin' him to mine."

"You keep your hands off of him, Jesse Wheat. Fristo's *my* man." He waved his arm wildly at Shag. "Shag Fristo, you come back here!"

Shag took his time about it, but he came.

Skinner said, "Looky here, Shag, I been lookin' for a man like you for twenty years. You ain't fired."

"I know it. I quit."

"You can't quit. I'll raise your wages. Forty dollars a month. There ain't no better in the country than that. And nothin' but gentle horses, either."

There wasn't a really gentle horse in the whole remuda, except the ones Skinner kept for himself. Shag scratched

14

his rust-colored head, then started to walk away from the group of men.

Jesse Wheat spoke up. "Wait now. We'll *both* hire you, me and Skinner. We'll need us a line cabin up here anyhow, and a rider to keep our cattle from gettin' all mixed up. I figure you'll be fair to both of us. We'll split your wages."

Shag chewed his lip and looked up at the cotton-puff clouds in the Texas sky. The fire and fight went out of him.

"Well, now, I might do that. But a line cabin's a two-man job. And it just so happens that I know a good man. . . ."

Yellow Devil

It was already an old kill when Jake Howard's three lion hounds found it. Jake clenched his teeth and futilely doubled a hard fist as he nudged aside with his boot toe the twigs, dead leaves, and bark that covered the carcass. He read the Lazy H brand on the stiffened hide of a two-year-old heifer.

"That yellow devil of a lion again," he muttered. The foreshoulders of the heifer were all but eaten away. The rest of the carcass had been expertly hidden, the mountain lion's way, and left to spoil.

Old Flop, Jake's lead hound, was eagerly nosing around for tracks. Another hound called Rip followed him. Little Mutt, Jake's pup in training, was sniffing at the carcass.

Jake lifted his stubbled chin and gazed bleakly toward the Carmen Mountains, which lay across the big bend of the Rio Grande. The fall air suddenly carried a chill. He closed up his old mackinaw, fumbling absently at the place where he had pulled off a button three weeks before and never had gotten around to fixing it.

"Give that old devil a little more time," Jake dismally spoke his thoughts aloud, "and he'll flat ruin me." The lion had already killed the kid crop from Jake's Angora goats, and some of the nannies as well. Now he was cultivating a taste for beef.

Presently Flop opened up and started barking "lion." Little Mutt raised his head, listening, then barreled off to follow the two older dogs.

Jake could tell by the way Flop was picking his way

16

up the side of the canyon that the trail was cold, had probably been there a week. But there was always the chance that by following it the dogs might cut a fresher trail. He swung up into the saddle and pulled the pack mule along behind him.

For hours the dogs struggled along with the trail, sniffing at the tops of rocks, going back and checking when the scent weakened. Finally the trail petered out for good in a heavily timbered header. Flop worked back and forth a long while before Jake reluctantly called him off.

Lions had a knack of doubling back over their own tracks, leaving a pack of confused dogs at what seemed to be the sudden end of a trail. Almost all lions were good at this, and the Yellow Devil was a master.

Desolately Jake shoved his hands deep into the pockets of his worn mackinaw and looked over at the ragged ridge of Big Bend mountains.

"I'd bet my boots he went yonderway, over onto Old Man Budge's ranch," he said to his dogs. "And they tell me the old coot's got a shotgun loaded with stock salt that he saves just to use on hunters."

The sun was edging down to where the trees on the mountains were throwing their shadows all the way across the canyon. The chill was working deeper into Jake's bones. He would have pulled his hounds in and headed back for the lonely old rock house he lived in if Flop hadn't struck a bear trail. It was fresh.

A lingering anger at the lion made Jake eager to catch something—anything—to help work off his frustration. Even if he hadn't wanted to, there wouldn't have been much he could do about it anyhow. His dogs had gone yonder. Their deep-throated belling sent a thrill up his spine as he spurred his horse and jerked the pack mule along. There was music in those voices, and a magic that only a hound-dog man could enjoy to its fullest.

It had been a good fall for Mexican black bears, drifting in from across the river. There were plenty of acorns and piñon nuts and berries. Jake knew this chase would make him lie out in the woods tonight. It would be too late to go back to the house. But the thought of good fresh bear meat instead of dry jerked beef munched along the trail made it seem worth the trouble.

Soon the hounds barked "treed" up ahead of him somewhere. Pulling in, Jake saw the dogs gathered at the bottom of a tree. Up in the top sat a bear, fat and ready for winter hibernation. Jake called the dogs back. He didn't want a wounded bear falling among his hounds and maybe ripping one open with his claws.

One shot was plenty. Skinning the bear, Jake whistled at the fat. Properly rendered, there was no grease in the world could beat good bear oil. Jake thought of Old Man Quincy Budge, and an idea struck him.

"They tell me there's no better way to work on a man than through his womenfolks," Jake said to inquisitive Little Mutt, who was still sniffing at the carcass. "And I think I got somethin' here that might do the job."

Soon after daylight Jake picked his way up to the head of a rock-rimmed canyon and the little huddle of adobe buildings that constituted Budge's headquarters. In an ocotillo-stalk corral stood half a dozen fine-looking horses. An old man was currying and brushing a blaze-faced sorrel. As he saw Jake dismount in front of the adobe house, he slipped the rope off the horse's neck, patted the animal, then came walking out to intercept the hunter.

Wood smoke curled out of the rock chimney, and the smell of it was pleasant in the sharp autumn air. Jake untied a canvas-wrapped bundle from the mule's back.

Old Man Quincy Budge stopped between Jake and the house and stood frowning, his feet wide apart. Budge had graying whiskers down to the collar. Jake thought idly that the old stockman would do well to curry his beard once in a while, the way he took care of his horses.

Jake was wary, but he managed a thin smile. "Mornin', Mr. Budge. I'm Jake Howard. I own the Lazy H."

He had met the old man a couple of times before, but Budge had never wasted much time trying to be friendly. He didn't now. He grunted and eyed Jake's dogs with open hostility.

A plump little woman shoved her head through the door. "Well, don't just stand there, Quincy. Invite the young man in to breakfast."

Budge grunted again and stood aside grudgingly. Moving past him, Jake tried to act as if he didn't notice Budge's animosity. Inside the kitchen, where the warmth clung to him like a wool coat, he laid down the bundle on the raw-topped plank table.

"Killed me a bear yesterday, Miz Budge. I wasn't far from here and thought you-all might enjoy havin' you some bear fat to render out. Can't beat it for good biscuits."

The old lady raised up both hands and chortled happily. She called, "Colleen, come in here and see what we've got."

A girl stepped into the kitchen from another room. Jake caught his breath short. She wore a loose cotton dress that almost swept the floor, and she was lithe and slender. Instinctively he reached up to his stubbled face and wished he had had some way to shave.

"Colleen," said Mrs. Budge, "this is Mr. Howard. Mr. Howard, our daughter."

Jake managed a smile and swallowed hard. Her eyes were big and fresh and brown. They studied him without shyness. Through breakfast Jake could feel the girl's gaze touching him. It made him so nervous, he couldn't eat but twelve flapjacks.

When Budge finished eating, he set his empty cup down in the saucer so hard it rang. He shoved his chair back on the rough board floor.

"Now then, Howard," he said gruffly, "I know you didn't come over here for no social call." He flicked a quick glance at his daughter. "Leastwise I don't think you did. What do you want?"

Jake was caught off guard, but there was no use in mincing words. "That yellow devil lion has been killin' my stock, Mr. Budge. I got a notion he comes over here when my dogs get to crowdin' him. I'd like your permission to hunt for him on your place."

The old man's heavy eyebrows knitted. His dark eyes

stared levelly at Jake. "They tell me you're more of a hunter than you are a stockman. They tell me you hunt varmints for pay, and that you furnish dogs and pack outfits to city hunters and guide them around for a fee."

Jake could feel the old man's answer coming. He nodded reluctantly.

Budge went on, his voice flat, "I'm a stockman myself. I like to work with cattle and horses. I got no patience with a man who spends his time out with guns and a pack of dogs when he ought to be home tendin' stock."

Angry warmth started rising in Jake. He could have told the old man why he hunted for pay. He could have told him that he had once owned a ranch bigger than the Lazy H and had it fully stocked with cattle. Then the drouth had come, and low prices, and a man couldn't fight them both. With what he could salvage he came up here to this smaller Lazy H with a handful of cattle, his mohair goats, and a big debt that had to be cleared up.

Hunting for a fee or guiding city hunters were ways of doing that. They paid expenses and left the ranch profit, if there was any, to apply on his debt.

He could have told Quincy Budge that. But stubborn anger was edging up in him, and he didn't say anything.

There was no compromise in Budge's voice. "Next time you come over here, you leave them guns at home. And don't you bring them flop-eared hounds with you no more either, or I'll chase the whole bunch of you back over the hill."

Jake went off vowing he wouldn't come back again. But for the next week or so the memory of a pair of big brown eyes stayed with him. And when he found himself in the vicinity of Budge's one day, he tied up his dogs and spurred off down the crooked trail to the ranch house. A couple of weeks later he did it again. Luckily old Quincy wasn't there. But Colleen was.

Jake was keeping close watch for the Yellow Devil to come back. So far, he and his dogs hadn't found any sign of the lion.

One day Doyle Short, a neighbor, rode into Jake's Lazy

H camp with his teenage son Tommy. Doyle swung down from his beat-up saddle and came walking up to Jake's little rock house, his face etched with worry.

"Jake," he said, "there's a bear been killin' my cattle. If you don't get him for me, he's goin' to cost me half my calf crop. What do you say to puttin' your dogs on him? It's worth fifty dollars to me if you get him."

Jake grinned. A man couldn't get rich that way, but fifty dollars would pay a lot of expenses.

Then Doyle sprang the catch. "I thought maybe you might let Tommy here go along and help you. I figure the experience would do him good."

Jake tried to keep from showing his misgivings. He had worked with Tommy on a couple of roundups. The boy was a little wild yet, and given to jumping before he looked to see where he was going to land.

Right now Tommy was sliding a rifle out of his saddle scabbard. He sighted down the barrel, straight toward Jake's horse corral. "You and your dogs jump him out for me, Jake. I'll shoot him right between the eyes."

Jake reached out and pulled down the muzzle of the rifle. "You better shove that back and leave it till you get somethin' to use it on."

He tried to hint to Doyle that he could handle the job better alone, but the hint didn't take. By afternoon he and the boy had the dogs sniffing around the bear's latest kill. It took only a minute for Flop to open up and head out with his nose close to the ground.

A couple of times young Tommy yelled excitedly, "I see him up there," and started hauling out his rifle. But he was mistaken, and Jake would make him put up the rifle. The trail meandered around considerably but was becoming fresher all the time. A little before sundown the dogs were getting excited. Jake figured the bear had heard them and was on the run.

They never came in sight of the killer. Even fat as he likely was, he was too fast for the hounds. When darkness came, Jake took out his old cow horn, called in the winded dogs, and set up camp.

21

As soon as it was light enough to see again, he turned the hounds loose on the trail. Finally the scent became hot. Once more the bear had heard them and was off in a hard run.

After a couple of hours the bear left Short's range and crossed the deadline claimed by Old Man Quincy Budge. Jake reined up and listened to his dogs going pell-mell along the trail.

"The old man'll have a fit if he finds out we're runnin' bear on his place," Jake said to the hard-breathing boy. "But it'd sure be hard to call the dogs off now."

He spurred on after them. The boy followed, his face flushed with excitement. The bear was looking for rough country.

Finally the sound of the dogs' barking changed.

"They got him treed, Tommy," Jake spoke quickly. "Let's catch up and get this done before Budge finds out we been here."

Flop, Rip, and Little Mutt had put the bear up a big spruce in a canyon not far from a whispering creek. Now the angry bear hunched in the limbs, his wide jaws apart.

Mouth open and eyes wide, the boy slipped his rifle out and raised it in shaky hands.

Alarmed, Jake said quickly, "Better steady that gun on a tree limb. You've got to make a clean kill."

But the boy didn't heed him. The rifle thundered. With a roar the wounded bear lost his hold. Limbs cracked as he fell. He hit the ground bawling and swinging his big paws. Instantly Little Mutt squatted and ran in at him.

Jake yelled at the dog, but it did no good. A vicious paw barely missed. The second time it sent the pup rolling, angry red claw streaks showing along his ribs. At the pup's sudden yelp of pain, the two older dogs started in.

In his mind Jake could see all three dogs cut to ribbons. He grabbed the rifle from the boy's hand and rushed in closer. For a moment he had to hold his fire to keep from hitting one of the dogs, which were rolling over and over with the bear. Then he got a clean bead. The recoil of the rifle jarred his shoulder.

The bear fell limp, and the dogs soon quieted down. Jake handed the rifle to pale, shaken young Tommy and ran to see about Little Mutt. The pup had some savage claw marks in his hide, but they weren't anything he wouldn't get over.

Jake jerked his head up as he heard Tommy yell shrilly, "It's another bear, Jake. I can see him over yonder."

Jake rose to his feet. "I don't think it's a bear, Tommy. Wait till we—"

He never finished. Steadying the rifle on a limb this time, Tommy fired before Jake could stop him. Jake's heart bobbed as he heard the animal's short scream.

"That's no bear!"

He sprinted as fast as his high-heeled boots would let him in the rocks. Lying in the brush, kicking out its last breath, he found a brown stallion. The Budge B brand was plain on the horse's hip—painfully plain.

Old Man Budge took it about as Jake had expected he would. He stormed like an angry bear. Jake couldn't blame him. The hunter knew he had it coming. Budge wouldn't even listen when Jake offered to pay for the stallion.

The old ranchman fetched a shotgun. "You better not let your shirttail touch you till you're off of my place, Howard. If you ever come back, I'll use this scattergun on you.

"And don't let them dogs come on my ranch again, neither. First thing I'm goin' to do in the mornin' is put out some strychnine baits. Bring them dogs again and there won't be a one of them git out alive!"

Jake backed away. Colleen tried to speak up for him, but the old man chopped off a few curt words to her and she stopped, her brown eyes full of sympathy for Jake. He gave her a long last glance, knowing that if he ever saw her again, it would have to be in spite of Quincy Budge. Then he got back on his horse and rode off, the hounds at heel.

As if that hadn't been hard luck enough, the Yellow Devil came back. A couple of mornings later the hounds turned up a fresh kill. It was another good heifer, a yearling this time. In less than a week Jake found where the lion had killed a bull calf and covered up its partially eaten carcass.

Always any attempt to track the lion was foiled. The Yellow Devil laid such tangled trails that sooner or later the dogs got balled up. Once Flop led the hounds successfully over a series of the lion's backtracks and kept on the trail. About midday the trail suddenly became hot. The hounds found a spot under a mountainside ledge where the lion apparently had been lying up through the day. Jake guessed the sound of the dogs had scared him into running again.

But the chase was all for nothing. In a couple of hours the trail led over the deadline and onto Budge's ranch. Bitterly Jake pulled up and started calling the dogs. It took a good while, but they reluctantly gave up the hot chase and came back.

Exhausted, Jake threw up his hands in despair and started home.

Winter came, and with it the Yellow Devil seemed hungrier than ever. One after another, Jake turned up fresh kills. Looking at his gradually shrinking herd, he knew he was ruined if he couldn't stop that lion. But he *couldn't* stop him.

So Jake's hatred for the Yellow Devil slowly grew stronger and stronger, until finally he worried no more about taking care of the ranch or the cattle. Only one thought rode in his mind—get that lion—one thought, day and night, week after desperate week.

Then one day it looked as if his luck would change. Following a fresh trail from the carcass of a calf, the hounds scared the Yellow Devil from a ledge so suddenly that the lion was a scant two hundred yards in the lead. As the hounds piled off the ledge, Jake caught a split-second look at the tawny shape before it disappeared in a tangle of brush across the canyon.

With a yelp of triumph Jake whipped the rifle out of his saddle scabbard and spurred his horse down the easiest way he could find to the canyon floor. By the time he reached bottom the dogs had disappeared into the brush. But their excited barking drifted back to him.

Shortly the trail went up the other side of the canyon. His mountain-trained horse climbed expertly but slowly. The sound of the dogs was farther away now, but maneuvering of the lion and necessary backtracking by the dogs allowed Jake to catch up. Almost before he realized it, he reached Budge's deadline.

He reined up a moment and mulled it over. This was the closest he had ever come to catching the Yellow Devil. If they were let go, the hounds might tree him at any time.

Jake remembered the old man's threat to use strychnine. But the sound of the dogs on a hot trail and the momentary glimpse of the hated killer had whipped him into a frenzied heat. Budge or no Budge, he was going to get that lion.

For an hour the dogs chased their prey across B Ranch land. The big cat was getting more desperate now, Jake knew from the trail. Jake sensed that he had driven the Yellow Devil off his usual range. The killer was on unfamiliar ground.

Suddenly Jake had a vague feeling something was wrong. He didn't know exactly what, but he sensed that one of his dogs had stopped barking. Loping up, he saw the reason.

Little Mutt lay on his side at the fork of a trail, his legs working feverishly, his eyes straining out of their sockets. His teeth were clamped tightly, biting into his tongue.

With a quick catch of breath, Jake exclaimed, "Strychnine!"

He could do nothing except stand there in misery and watch the pup die. He kept blowing the old cow horn until the other two dogs finally came trotting in, their tongues lolling out. Their accusing eyes said they could have treed the lion if only he had let them.

Choking, Jake put leash chains on the two dogs and led them away. Old Flop kept looking up at the dead pup in the saddle and whimpering.

With a deep bitterness creeping through him, Jake turned his back on the Yellow Devil and headed for the shortest trail off the B Ranch. He blinked his stinging eyes. He berated the lion. He lambasted the ornery old man who would let a killer lion lie up on his range but put out strychnine to poison faithful hounds.

As it turned out, the chase had not been a complete failure. The Yellow Devil did not come back to the Lazy H.

Jake wondered about this. Then reports started coming in. The lion was killing Quincy Budge's horses.

Jake reasoned that the many chases his hounds had given the lion, capped off by the final one that had come so close, had scared the Yellow Devil off his home range. Now the cat had found something he liked better—good, tender, easy-to-kill colts.

Week after week, reports came in. Budge had lost more than half of his last colt crop. The lion seldom returned to old kills now. With horseflesh plentiful, every time he got hungry, he made a new kill.

Time and again Budge had moved the horses, but always the Yellow Devil followed them. The old man had lain out in the biting cold night after bitter night, hoping to get a shot at the killer. The chance never came. But every time he missed a night, another horse would die.

Folks said Quincy Budge had aged ten years in the two months the Devil had been working on him. Contrary though he was, he loved those horses. But Jake hadn't seen the old rancher. A couple of times he got word Budge was coming over to talk to him. He would leave his ranch then and camp out a night or two, until he figured the old man had come and gone.

But one day Budge caught him unawares. He rode up to the barn while Jake was feeding Flop and Rip and a new pup he was training to take Little Mutt's place. Looking at the old man, Jake felt a bit sorry for him, though he tried not to. The lines in Budge's bearded face were carved deeper than ever. His eyes were like those of a whipped dog.

"Look, Howard," the old man pleaded, "if that lion works on me much longer, I'm through. I ain't done nothin' for two months but hunt for him. I've hired men with dogs to try and track him, but their dogs ain't like yours."

Jake kept his voice flat. "I'm surprised you could get anybody to take dogs in there, seein' as how you've put out strychnine."

The old man flinched. "I knew where I put them baits, Howard. I went out and took them all up."

"All of them?"

Guilt showed in Budge's lined face. "All but one. I heard about it, Howard. My wife and daughter jumped me good when the word came about your dog. . . . I'm tellin' you, I'm sorry about the pup. It was spite made me do it. I've thought it over aplenty since. I'm askin' you to forgive me, Howard, and help me git that lion."

Jake wanted to. He still hated the Yellow Devil as much as he ever had. But there was a stubbornness about him.

He looked at the sinking sun. "It'll be dark before you get home if you don't get started." He turned his back and walked off.

"Wait, Howard," Budge called desperately, "I'll give you a hundred dollars—two hundred—to catch that cat."

Jake hesitated. Two hundred dollars. That would pay for a good many losses. But no, he wouldn't back down now. He kept walking.

Next day another rider came. Jake recognized Colleen Budge, and his heart quickened. He knew what she wanted. He was determined to turn her down.

But that was not easy to do. "Dad's not a bad man at heart," she pleaded. "It hurt him when he heard about your pup, knowin' it was his fault. You can't imagine what that lion's done to him. It's killin' him. I'm beggin' you to come track down that lion—for me."

He felt his face coloring as he realized he was whipped. "All right. I'll do it."

She kissed him, and the warmth was still with him long after she had gone.

That night Jake took his dogs, horse, and pack mule over to Budge's ranch, to be ready to start the hunt at daylight the next morning. Quincy Budge was pacing the kitchen floor, blowing at his steaming coffee cup and raring to go an hour before pink light began to creep over the great wall of the Carmens to the east. Jake had little to say to him.

Colleen put on a long riding skirt and went along with them. Soon after sunup they were at the site of the latest slaughter. The dogs sniffed around a freshly killed sorrel colt while Budge sat stiffly in his saddle. Jake saw tears in the old man's eyes.

As usual, old Flop was the hound that opened and led out. The trail followed a winding course but continued strong. The colt's blood on the cat's paws was making him easier for the dogs to track.

Finally the trail seemed to come to a dead end along a rimrock. Flop patiently worked the back trail, his nose rubbing raw on the rocks.

Jake looked over the rim and spotted a tall tree not far below. It gave him a hunch. He called Flop and let him sniff around the edge. Surely enough, he picked up the scent just above the tree. The lion had backtracked, then jumped off into the tree. He wasn't in it now. He must be down there somewhere in the steep-walled canyon.

"I'm takin' the dogs and goin' down afoot," he said. "You-all can keep the horses up here on the rim. Just listen for the dogs and follow them."

Quincy Budge climbed stiffly out of the saddle. "I'm goin' with you."

Jake warned, "It's rough goin' down there afoot. And there's no tellin' how far we might have to run him."

The old man grunted. "It's my horses he's been killin'. Let's go."

It was a tough, dangerous climb down the steep walls. They had to hand the hounds down part of the way. The old man slipped once, bruising his knee against a sharp rock and ripping a hole in his pant leg. But he never seemed to notice it. A grim look had hardened in his eyes.

The hounds picked up the scent at the bottom of the tree and headed out up the canyon again. Jake fell in behind them in a long trot, his rifle balanced in his hand. He wondered how long Budge would be able to keep up.

The old man surprised him. He seldom lagged far behind. Occasionally, where sand had blown into ripples, a lion track was visible. That would bring new life into the old man's steps. But the dogs paid no particular attention to tracks. They kept right on by scent.

The trail led up onto a ledge. There the scent seemed especially hot. The Yellow Devil had been lying up there, Jake figured, until the sound of the dogs had scared him away. He looked off down the canyon as if he hoped for a glimpse of the fleeing lion. But he saw nothing.

Even the pup had the scent now. All three dogs were tearing ahead, fast enough to outrun a good horse and far too fast for men afoot to keep up with them. But Jake did his best. He ran until his heart was like a lead weight in him. He glanced back occasionally. Quincy Budge labored heavily along, falling farther and farther back but not quitting.

Jake's hatred of the cat returned to him now. The tom's trail angled over to the canyon wall again. For a minute it was lost. Then Flop tracked back to where the lion had made a long jump up onto a boulder the size of a small shack. Jake boosted the dog to where he could clamber up on the rock. The scent was there, all right. Jake handed the other dogs up.

The lion had jumped onto another ledge overhead. Again Jake had to lift the dogs up. They seemed heavy as horses now, even the pup, which he put up last. He struggled to pull himself up after them.

The trail led on and on, across jagged rock ledges, back down to the canyon floor, then up again. Jake's mouth and throat were dry. His heart hammered dully. His breath came short and painfully. At times he wanted to call the dogs off. But the sound of them ahead of him kept pulling him on. Still, he knew he could not go much farther. It had to end soon now, or the chase was lost.

The dogs' voices faded thin. Jake stopped and leaned on a tree to regain his breath. His heart bobbed as he recognized the gliding shape creeping up across the rocks. The Yellow Devil had momentarily thrown the dogs again on a double-back. Now he was trying to sneak out of the canyon.

In desperation Jake realized the chase was over if the cat did get out. The hunter didn't have strength left to climb that wall. He raised his rifle and took a long shot. He heard the bullet ricochet off a rock over the lion's head and whine away. The cat whirled back like a whiplash and leaped once more into the canyon.

He disappeared into the brush. Jake heaved on after him. This time, he knew, the hunt would be finished. There was no deadline to worry about, no place beyond which he could not go. He would trail the Yellow Devil into Mexico now, if he had to.

But he wouldn't have to. A new, excited note came into the dogs' voices. They had jumped the lion. Fatigue was a lance shoved through Jake's ribs, but he made himself keep on. He heard the hounds bark "treed."

Flushed with victory, Jake made his weary legs move a little faster. Most of the pain left his chest. He saw the dogs ahead, one after another rearing up onto the trunk of a tall spruce and barking. High in the branches, a tawny form crouched on a limb.

The Yellow Devil.

He was cornered now. He did not stand a chance. But there was a majesty about him as he sat high in the tree, looking down, never taking his eyes off the dogs. His ears were laid back. He spat defiantly at the hounds that had treed him.

But Jake wasn't thinking of the majesty of the beast. He remembered dead cattle—his cattle—and goats he had found where the lion left them. He remembered long, weary chases that led always to disappointment. He remembered a brown pup named Little Mutt.

A choking hatred surged in him, and he raised his rifle. He drew a careful bead on the Yellow Devil. But his hands wavered, and he thought of an old man trudging wearily along the trail back yonder, an old man who had lain out in misery night after night, who had not been able to keep the tears out of his eyes as he looked down at a dead colt.

He remembered Quincy Budge and the hard lines that had edged into his face. In the last two months the tom had become more than a stock-killing cat to Budge. It had been almost a human enemy, an enemy to be hated and hunted, and if possible destroyed, before he destroyed the old man.

For months Jake had dreamed of this moment. Now he had the rifle in his hand and the lion in a tree. He told himself he owed Budge nothing.

But reluctantly he lowered his rifle, the taste of victory sour in his mouth. This shot belonged to Quincy.

Colleen got there before Quincy did. Leading the horses and mule along the rim of the canyon, she had followed the sound of the dogs. When she heard them bark "treed," she spurred ahead to a break in the rimrock and came down.

She found Jake waiting there, rifle in his hands. She was watching when Jake handed Quincy the rifle and turned away.

Jake flinched at the slap of the gunshot. Limbs popped as the dead tom fell. Jake turned and watched the dogs, especially the new pup, wooling the lion's body around at the base of the tree.

Quincy Budge's face slowly relaxed. The lines in it seemed to soften a little. The sag was gone from his shoulders.

Colleen touched Jake's hand. "You wanted to make that shot yourself. Thanks for lettin' Dad do it."

"He's payin' me two hundred dollars," Jake said.

She smiled. "You know that's not it, Jake."

Jake nodded and took the hand she extended toward him. "I reckon it isn't." He looked at the dead lion. "I'm not mad at anybody anymore. Or anything."

He caught the mule and led him up to the Yellow Devil. Time they packed this lion it would be time to get started. It was a long way home.

That 7X Bull

That old motley-faced bull bellowing his arrogant way up and down the caprock country was about all that was left to show for the sprawling 7X outfit. The 7X had been burned onto his roan-colored hip in the last fall branding before the receivers took over. They sold the rest of the cattle and scattered them all over hell and half of Texas. But nobody ever smeared a loop on old 7X again. His horns were mossy now from age, and his red-flecked hide was scarred from scores of fights which had all ended the same way.

Old 7X was a holdout of the longhorn strain. True, his sire had been a white-faced Hereford brought in to deepen the bodies and shorten the legs of the rangy Texas cattle. But 7X had taken after his mammy, a waspy old outlaw long of horn and leg, short of patience and temper.

I said the bull was *about* all there was left. Dodge Willingham was still around too. He was on the off side of sixty, spare and dried as a strip of jerked beef. He'd been with the 7X outfit ever since they'd trailed their first longhorn cattle up from the South Texas brush country. There hadn't been any barbed wire then, and a man whose luck played out could still lose his scalp under a bloody Comanche moon.

After the bust-up, Dodge had stayed on with the new Bar J, which had bought out the headquarters division of the 7X.

Dodge and the big bull had a right smart in common. They were both throwbacks to a time that was gone. And they were fighters, the both of them. Every so often an old restlessness got to riding Dodge, like the time in Midland he decided a saloon was too quiet for his taste. He hollered disgustedly, "What is this, a church?" and tipped a table full of cards and poker chips into the players' laps. They beat the whey out of him. Dodge had a wonderful time.

He was an old hand when I first knew him. I was just a raw young kid who wanted to walk in his footsteps, but mostly he acted like he didn't know I was there.

I'll never forget the spring day the Bar J foreman dropped in at our dugout line camp. Ellison Finch was Old Man Johnson's son-in-law. Finch never wanted you to forget who the boss was. He jerked his thumb at Dodge's .30–.30 rifle on its pegs over the door.

"Dodge," he said, "I've took all I'm goin' to from that old red roan bull. He's killed a dozen of my . . . of the ranch's good bulls, and he's chased off plenty of others. He's sired more scrawny wild calves than me and you could both count. Now I want you to take that gun and go find him. Spend a week if you got to, but find him. And make almighty sure he's dead before you ride away."

Dodge's pale gray eyes seemed to glisten as he looked up at the gun. His horny fist knotted up hard as a live-oak stump.

"Looky here, Finch," he spoke after a long minute, "old 7X has been around a long time. He ain't got much longer to go. Why don't you just leave him be?"

When he had been an ordinary thirty-a-month cowboy like the rest of us, Finch had stood in awe of Dodge. Now he had married into the order-giving class. He glared a hole through the aging cowpuncher.

"That old bull has outlived his time," Finch said. "He's a nuisance, even a hazard. If you won't kill him, I'll get me somebody that will."

After Finch left, Dodge walked out to the barn to sit and brood. He stayed there till dark, and I knew better than to go bother him. In my own mind I was already grown. But to Dodge Willingham I was still just a button and supposed to keep quiet. Next morning he took the .30–.30 and rode out. About suppertime he was back, his mouth a straight, hard line. He barely spoke a word for a week.

Old 7X was never mentioned again until the fall roundup. The wagon was camped at Comanche Wells on the caprock the day Dodge failed to come in on drive. We went on with the branding and cutting out of long-age cattle to push to the railroad. But all the time we kept looking over our shoulders. Late in the afternoon we saddled fresh horses and started out to search.

We met Dodge walking in, a mile from camp. His clothes were torn and smeared with blood. The side of his face was skinned like he'd slid down a mountain on his ear.

"That old dun stumbled on a slope and broke his neck," he told Finch. "Taken me an hour to work my saddle off of him. I carried it a good ways and left it where I could find it again."

I noticed that Dodge looked at the ground as he talked. He had always been able to stare the devil straight in the eye and spit on him. Something in his voice didn't ring true. I knew. But Finch took Dodge at his word. That is, till we got the old puncher back to the wagon and stretched him out on his tarp-covered bedroll. We took the blood-smeared shirt off of him. Finch stared in wonder at Dodge's wound. Anger boiled into his sun-blistered face.

"That gash you've got there . . . I know a horn tip when I see one. Did you shoot that 7X bull like I told you to?"

Dodge knew he was caught. You could tell by the sick look that wiped across his stubbled face.

Finch bent over him, his fingers stuck out stiff as wagon spokes. "I ought to fire you, Dodge. I would, if I didn't know the old man'd raise hell. Now that bull's sired him another crop of mean, scrubby calves. You ought to've shot him. We'll bring him in now. We'll tie a clog to his foot and drag him in if we have to. He'll go to market with the steers and wind up as sausage. Before it's over, you'll wish you'd killed him."

Anybody else would just send another cowboy out to

kill the bull and say nothing more. But Finch wanted Dodge to know who the boss was.

Dodge didn't seem to be worried much. I guess he knew the old outlaw too well. "I jumped 7X up there close to the bluffs," he told us later. "I thought I'd run him off away from the drive so nobody would see him. But before I could hardly move, he'd rammed a horn right through that dun. I like to've not got away from there myself."

Even then you could hear the pride in Dodge's voice. "What I mean, boys, he's a fighter. Ain't many of us left."

For the next few days Finch would detail a few punchers to go and try to bring old 7X in. The results were always the same. Some of the hands never got close enough to see anything of the bull except his south end going north. Others caught up with him and wished they hadn't. The rest of us went on with the regular roundup work. Finch had taken Dodge out of the saddle and put him to swamping for the wagon cook—washing up the utensils, shagging in the wood.

One day two cowboys came walking in from the bluffs, leading their half-crippled horses. Finch blew up and left camp, talking to himself. When he came back two days later he brought two mean-looking dogs with him.

"Cow dogs," he said, his gloating eyes resting on Dodge.

Dodge snickered. "Old 7X'll tear up them pups like a lobo wolf does a jackrabbit."

Finch shook his head. "You're goin' with us tomorrow, Dodge. I want you to see this."

I felt sorry for Dodge as I watched Finch walk out toward the remuda. Dodge had never seen cow dogs work. I had. I'd repped for the Bar J one time when the Rafter D's had used them to jump outlaw cattle down out of the rough country.

We quartered north from camp next morning and came upon a wild steer we had missed somehow.

"Watch him, Dodge," Finch said. He spoke to the trailing dogs. They went bounding after the steer, faster than a horse could run. It went so quick we hardly saw how it happened. The biggest dog darted in and grabbed the steer's nose with his teeth. Somehow he swung his body between the animal's forelegs. The steer went crashing to the grass-matted ground. He got up and ran again, only to be thrown once more.

For the first time, the confidence began to drain out of Dodge's face. Worry settled into his smoke-gray eyes.

The bluffs and the rough, broken country around them had been old 7X's favorite running grounds ever since his snaky mammy had first stood over him, licking him clean and giving him his first bellyful of warm milk to steady those wobbly legs. There, except for the year he had been a calf, he had showed his heels to cowboys every time they went after him.

Strange tales about him had grown by the dozen. And a bright light always flickered in the eyes of old cowboys like Dodge Willingham as they told those tales around crackling mesquite campfires, or by dancing yellow lamplight in a smoky bunkhouse. Old 7X represented a time when they had been young like us, when a man could still glory in the wildness of the country and all the creatures on it.

We found where the big roan bull had been watering in a low swale which always caught the runoff from the rains. Tracks showed there might be a couple of cows with him. Excitement began to flush Finch's heavy face. His hands kept rubbing his leather chaps as we worked along the edge of the bluffs.

We rode upon one of the cows first. She was a rangy, high-tailed old sister that showed her Hereford blood only in her markings. Her long legs carried her clattering down a slope with the speed of an antelope. One of the cowboys spurred after her. Finch called him back.

"Let her go. It's the bull we want."

Old 7X spotted us first. We saw him break from a small clump of mesquite and take out in a high lope for the broken ground that lay to the south. Whatever else his age might have done, it hadn't slowed his speed.

Finch hollered like a half-grown kid and socked spurs to the sorrel horse he rode. We fell in behind him. Even

Dodge, reluctant as he was, stayed right up with the bunc
We didn't get within shouting distance of old 7X till he we
sliding down the steep side of a hill, taking a shower
small rocks with him.

Down past the crest of the next hill waited the bluf
It wasn't but a minute or two till we had old 7X ringed i
The only way out for him was down the face of a cliff. I
stood looking at us in anger and contempt, his long ta
arched, his horned head proud and high, jerking from on
of us to the other. He decided the foolishness had gone of
long enough. He lowered that great head and came chargir
like the locomotive on a Santa Fe freight. Every one of u
except Dodge had our ropes down and our cinches haule
up tight. But the sight of that snorting old bull bearir
down on us made us forget everything except to get out
his way. We could hear Finch shouting at us, but he didr
sound nearly so mean as that bull.

Old 7X roared through the line and kept going. I wouldr
have given a plugged nickel for anybody's chance of catchir
him.

But Finch didn't quit. He sicced the dogs after the ol
roan. They must have run a quarter of a mile before the
finally caught up. He slid to a stop and turned to face then
those sharp horns down. He made a quick pass at the smalle
of the dogs. I heard the dog yelp as a horn glanced off h
lanky rump.

The older dog knew his business. He jumped in an
clamped his sharp teeth on 7X's long ear. The bull roare
and shook his head violently. The dog had to let go. Th
bull lunged at him, but the dog scooted out of the way
The younger dog leaped in and tried at 7X's other ear bu
missed. Then the big dog got hold of the bull's nose. Th
smaller dog tried again, and this time he grabbed the ear

Old 7X pitched and bellowed, the dogs staying wit
him. The two were trying to pull him down, but he wa
too heavy.

We reined up and watched, hardly knowing whethe
to believe it or not. Even as 7X fought his hardest, we kne
he was licked.

Old Dodge was licked too. Never had I seen the hope-lessness that had sunk into his wind-carved face. I wished I could help him. But what was there a button could say?

Cruel pleasure glowed in Finch's face. His eyes fairly glittered with the pride of doing something nobody else had done.

"For God's sake, Finch," Dodge pleaded, "call them dogs off of him. Ain't you got a drop of human blood left in you?"

"We'll call off the dogs when we get our ropes on that old hellion."

Finch rode in close and dropped a small loop over the outlaw's horns. "Somebody else tie on," he said. "We don't want him bustin' our ropes loose."

Johnny Tisdale dabbed another loop over 7X's horns. A third rider worked around and heeled the bull. They rode off in opposite directions. Stretched out, the old roan fought for balance, then heaved over onto his side with the solid thump of a boulder smacking into mud. The dogs let go. They moved off and faced around to watch, their lank sides heaving, their tongues lolling out.

Finch turned his horse over to another cowboy to keep the rope tight. He swung down, his big Chihuahua spurs jingling. He cut his grinning eyes toward Dodge, then away again. He was taking his time, letting Dodge get the full benefit of this. Finch walked to a mesquite tree and whittled off a limb to about three feet in length. Notching one end, he tied it to the bull's huge right forefoot with a pigging string.

"Now, old bull," he said, "let's see how you run with this clog on you."

Finch trotted back to his horse. The moment the bull felt the ropes slacken he jumped to his feet, head down in challenge. He tried to paw dirt and felt the clog drag. He shook the foot, but the long stick still hung there.

With a bellow he charged at one of the horses. The first long step shook the heel rope off his hind feet, but two ropes were still fastened around his horns. He tripped on the clog and plunged to the ground. He got up again, shaking his head. It was then that I noticed for the first time that his left eye was gone. He had probably lost it in some bruising battle here among these bluffs.

Old 7X tried to charge again, but the same thing happened to him. Time and again he would get up, hind feet first, and once more the clog would send him crashing down. Finch would let the dogs rush in and grab him to add to the bull's misery.

Feeling humiliated myself, I knew how this must be affecting Dodge. "Come on, Dodge," I said, pulling my horse around. "What say we go back to the wagon?"

He shook his head, anger building in his eyes.

Old 7X gave up at last, his muscles quivering from fatigue. I expected him to sull, to refuse to move. But that in itself would have been a form of surrender.

Finch said, "All right, boys, let's take him in."

Ropes still on his horns, they started the bull toward the wagon. Every time he faltered, the dogs grabbed at his heels. Every time he tried to run, the clog stopped him. Finch had won.

As we rode in we found the rest of the hands working the day's gather in the plank corrals. The roan bull began to bellow at the sight and sound of the other cattle. Finch and Johnny led him through a gate. Finch pulled up and grinned.

"Here you are, you old scorpion. Next stop's a sausage grinder."

They had to heel him and throw him down again to get the ropes off. Then Finch left him in a tiny pen with a bunch of long-age steers and gave us all plenty to do. The last I saw of old 7X for a while, he was hooking irritably at the unlucky steers that had to share the small space with him. If it weren't for the clog, he would go over that fence like it wasn't there and be back in the bluffs before the dust was well settled.

After we ate supper, we went to the corrals to brand the calves dropped since the last roundup. Catching my breath while waiting for a heeler to drag up another calf, I sighted Dodge slipping around behind the corral where old

7X was. The bull had quieted down and stood beside the plank fence. I saw Dodge look around quickly, then take a knife out of his pocket, kneel down and reach under the bottom plank. In a moment he came bowlegging it back, satisfaction in his grizzled face.

After the branding, Finch sent most of the hands out to push the herd far back on to the south end of the ranch. That way the freshly worked cattle weren't so apt to get caught again in the next few days' gather. Most of the outfit gone, Finch walked to the small corral where 7X was. "Turn him out in the trap with the steers," he said. "He ain't a-goin' to do much with that clog on him."

Johnny Tisdale opened the gate to let the steers out of the little pen into a bigger one. Old 7X waited until the rest of the cattle were out before he budged. Then, with resignation, he moved slowly toward the gate.

Suddenly he stopped and shook his right forefoot. The clog was gone. He stood there as if he was trying to puzzle the thing out. Then he shook that great head, lowered it, and came on the run.

Finch just had time to let out a startled yelp and hit the fence. He climbed it three planks at a time. The rest of us weren't far behind him. I glimpsed Dodge standing off to one side, laughing fit to bust. The bull made a beeline for the outside gate. He tried to jump it but splintered the top two planks like matchsticks.

Our horses were tied outside, up and down the fence. At the sight of that monster of a bull bearing down on them they snorted in panic and popped bridle reins right and left. In seconds every horse was loose, and every one of us was left afoot. Unable to move, we just stood there and watched while old 7X headed for the bluff country in a high lope.

A mule skinner would have blushed if he could have seen Finch tear the hat from his head and stomp on it and could have heard the things Finch said. When he finally ran out of cusswords in English and had used up the few Spanish ones he knew, Finch walked over and picked up the clog. Anybody could tell it had been cut. He stomped

40

out of the pen, his raging eyes fixed on Dodge. His fists were knotted, his jaws bulging out.

"You damned old reprobate, you'll wish you'd left this country ten years ago!"

Dodge didn't back away. When I saw Finch was going to hit him, I stepped between them. I was getting mad myself. "Better take a dally on that temper, Finch," I said. "Lay a hand on Dodge and you'll have to whip me too."

Dodge caught my shoulder and roughly pushed me aside. "Keep out of it, button!"

My feelings were hurt by the old man's rebuff. Finch's eyes brimmed with fury. "You're fired, the both of you, and I don't care what Old Man Johnson says about it. Either I'm the boss here or I ain't."

Dodge just shrugged. "I'd done decided to quit anyhow. This is no place for a *man* to work."

We stayed there that night because it was too late to leave the wagon. All Dodge would say to me was, "You sure ripped your britches, boy."

Next morning we watched the hands rope their horses out of the remuda. Finch was taking about half the crew to the bluffs. He swore he was going to get that bull today and get him alive. He stopped for one last dig at Dodge.

"He won't get away this time. We'll use the dogs again. And once we catch him, he'll tame down quick. I'm goin' to take the pride out of him." He pulled out his knife, holding it up for Dodge to see.

Dodge brought up his gnarled fist and drove it into Finch's face. A trickle of blood worked down from Finch's nose. Dodge crouched to do it again, but I caught his arm. Finch brought up his fists, looking first at Dodge and then at me. He turned around, climbed into the saddle, and led out in a stiff trot, his back arrow straight.

We watched the riders move away as daylight fanned out across the rolling short-grass country. Dodge saddled his horse, jerking at the cinch harder than was necessary. Finished, he led him toward the chuckwagon. Grim purpose came into his face as he wrapped the reins around a mesquite limb a proper distance from the cookfire. He reached up into the wagonbed and pulled out a rifle that the cook kept there.

The cook's jaw sagged. "Good God, Dodge, they'll hang you!"

The same thought had hit me, and the pit of my stomach was like ice.

Dodge shook his head. "I ain't after Finch. He ain't worth what it'd cost me." Sadness settled over him. "Looks like old 7X has finally got to go. But he deserves better than what Finch'll give him. At least he ought to be allowed to die respectable." He turned to me. "Comin', boy?"

Dodge swung into the saddle and spurred out in the lead, rifle across his lap. We skirted east a ways, to be out of sight of Finch and the other punchers. Then we moved into an easy lope and held it. After a while we knew we were ahead, for even in anger Finch would keep his horses in a sensible trot to save their strength.

When we got to the bluffs we climbed up high and looked behind us. We saw no sign of Finch. That gave us a little time to find old 7X first. We needed it. It took us the better part of an hour before we finally saw the old patriarch trying to hide himself in a clump of mesquite brush. We eased down toward him, our horses alert, their ears poking forward like pointing fingers. Seeing that we had spotted him, 7X bolted out of the thicket, popping brush like a buffalo stampede. But there was a bad limp to his right forefoot.

"Damned clog done that to him," Dodge muttered. He spurred up. The bull saw he couldn't outrun us, and he faced around. He tossed his head.

Dodge's Adam's apple worked up and down as he levered a cartridge into the chamber. He raised the rifle to his shoulder, held it there a moment, then slowly let it down. His hands trembled.

"I can't do it. I'd sooner put a bullet in Finch."

Right then old 7X decided to fight his way out. He charged. Dodge whipped the rifle up, but panic had grabbed his horse. The big gray boogered to one side, and Dodge tumbled out of the saddle. The rifle roared. The bullet exploded a brown puff of dust from the ground.

My heart was in my mouth; 7X was almost upon Dodge, and there wasn't any place for the old puncher to jump. I spurred up beside Dodge and grabbed at his shoulders. In desperation he dug his fingers into my leg, trying to pull up beside me. I managed to swing my horse around to protect Dodge. But 7X's huge head plowed into my dun's haunches. The horse fell.

I landed on top of Dodge. We both jumped to our feet, but we were too late to grab the bridle reins. My horse ran away. We stood there with our backs to the steep bluff. Not a solitary thing could we see to grab onto or a place to climb.

As old 7X whirled around to fasten his good eye upon us, I saw Dodge's rifle lying in the dust. So scared I could hardly breathe, I grabbed it. Somehow I managed to lever another cartridge into place as the great roan bull bellowed and came at us.

There wasn't time to aim. I jammed the rifle butt to my shoulder and squeezed the trigger, my teeth biting halfway through my lip. Old 7X went down on his knees. The bullet had glanced off just above the right eye. He staggered to his feet again. He stood shaking that huge head in pain. Blood trickled down from the wound.

Dodge saw the trouble as soon as I did. "By George, that blood has blinded him."

Hearing Dodge's voice, the bull stopped shaking his head. In one last wild charge, he lunged blindly at the sound of the man he hated. We jumped out of his way, and he kept running.

At the edge it seemed he stopped dead still for a second. Then he was gone, plunging down off the sheer face of the bluff. I heard Dodge gasp. From below came the crashing sound of impact.

It took us a while to catch our boogered horses and work our way down to the base of the bluff. We found the mossy-horned old bull lying there just as he had landed.

Life was gone from the battle-scarred body. I saw the glistening in Dodge's gray eyes. The old puncher knelt and traced with his finger the dim outline of an ancient 7X brand on the roan hip.

"I put that brand there myself, a long time ago." He was silent a while, remembering. "But times change, and things that won't change have got to go. Old 7X and me, we stayed beyond our day." He straightened and gazed a long while across the rolling short-grass country to the south of us, the old 7X range. "He went out in a way that was fittin' to him. He fought every last step of it."

I held my silence as long as I could. "We better be movin' on, Dodge. Finch'll be along directly."

Dodge squatted stiffly on his spurred heels and began rolling a cigarette, making it plain he was going to wait. "Old 7X left here a-fightin'. So will I."

"But you don't really think you can whip Finch, do you?"

Dodge shrugged. "I'll never know till I try." He turned up his tough old face and glanced at me with that brimstone look in his eyes. "If it turns out *I* can't whip him, I expect *you're* man enough to."

I knew then that I wasn't just a button anymore.

Jailbreak

Some people claim they can tell a lawman as far as they can see him. Grant Caudell was not a lawman, but he had the look of one about him as he trotted his sorrel horse into the dusty, lamplit street of Twin Wells. It had been a long ride, a relentless search that had driven a deep weariness into his bones and put a heavy slump in his wide shoulders. But his stubbled jaw still kept a grim, determined set. And he sensed somehow that his search was done, that he had at last caught up with Slack Vincent.

An undefined tension hung in the air, taut and ominous. Grant Caudell caught its electric tingle as he eased his horse along among the scattered knots of men. He felt it in the way they stood together quietly, saying little to each other except in muttered undertones that did not carry beyond their tight circles.

Most stood with eyes fixed on the ground, or on their rough hands, or on the warped planks of the splintered, tobacco-stained sidewalks. Seldom did they look up into each other's faces, made unnaturally grave by deep shadows from the lamplight.

Far up the street Caudell made out the shape of a frame jail, its barred front starkly illuminated by lanterns hung over its short porch. Before it three men stood with guns in their hands and stolidly kept watch on the street.

It was as if the whole town waited for some signal, some spark. A shudder worked up between Caudell's shoulder blades, adding bleakness to a face already pinched and wrinkling from forty years in the hot sun and the dry wind of Texas.

He reined up at the livery barn and stiffly swung down. The old livery hand stood in the wide door, smelling of sour whisky and dry hay and unwashed horse sweat.

"What's happened here?" Caudell asked the whiskered, dusty man.

"Fixin' to be a hangin'," came the reply in a quick, eager voice. "Soon's that bunch of folks from the L4 gits in here. Sheriff thinks he can stop it, but he's got another think comin'."

Dull dread settled in Caudell. "What's it all about?"

A slight stir down the street made the little man step forward in expectation. The stir died, and he slumped back, disappointed. "Feller held up the bank today. Girl in there got hysterical and run for the door. He shot her.

"They caught him before he got a mile out of town. They'd've strung him up right there if the sheriff hadn't been so quick. But they'll git him tonight, don't you doubt it."

Grant Caudell's heart quickened in dismay. "This robber—what did he look like?"

"Tall feller, stooped a little, got gray eyes that drive through you like a tenpenny nail. Scar low on his cheek. Regular killer if ever I seen one. And," he added proudly, "I've seen a many of them." The description couldn't fit anyone but Slack Vincent.

Caudell felt sick at his stomach. For five months he had hunted Slack Vincent, trailing him up into Kansas, then all the way back into Texas, from cow outfit to cow outfit, from one gambling hall and fancy place to another. Now, at last, he had found him. And a lynch mob had first call!

Grant left his sorrel hitched to somebody's picket fence near the back of the jail. If a mob did come, he reasoned, there was no use letting it booger his horse clear out of the country.

Quickly, his spurs ringing to the hurried strike of his boots, he strode around to the jail's front. Instantly three shotguns were shoved into his face. Purposeful, worried-looking men stood behind them. Lantern light struck a reddish reflection from a badge.

"I've got to see the sheriff, quick," Caudell said.

The shotguns eased back a little, but one of the men shook his head. "Now? Look, friend, you'd better drift before this pot comes to a boil."

Caudell held his ground. "It's about your prisoner. I think I know him."

One of the deputies leaned forward to peer distrustfully into Caudell's face. "Go on in, then, but leave us your pistol. And you'd better make it quick. When the L4's hit town there's goin' to be hell. That was Old Man Longley's daughter he killed."

The sheriff was middle-aged, not many years older than Caudell. Troubled lines were etched deeply under his tired blue eyes, and his stubbled face sagged in weariness. He stared at Caudell with incredulity. "You say you want to speak to the prisoner? There's a mob gatherin' out yonder. They want to speak to him too."

A clock was ticking in Caudell's mind, and he knew it was almost time for the alarm to go off. "I'll tell it to you quick, Sheriff. His name is H. W. Vincent. They call him Slack. I hired him to help me with a bunch of cattle we trailed up to the railhead. Everything I owned was ridin' on those steers. Even my wife's dad and mother had all their money in them.

"When I got the cattle sold, Vincent shot me in the back and rode off with the money. I was laid up in bed for sixty days before I could even climb on a horse. As soon as I could ride, I took up his trail. I've been on it for five months. Now I've got to talk to him before that mob gets here. If he's still got any of our money left, hidden someplace, I've got to get him to tell me."

The sheriff studied him thoughtfully, plainly not entirely believing. "All right," he said, his reluctance strong, "but you'd better be quick. I'm afraid there ain't much time."

Caudell frowned. "You goin' to let that bunch have him?"

The sheriff's voice was bitter. "Not without a fight. But I ain't goin' to kill any of my friends to save *him*."

He led Caudell back through a narrow, short corridor. He stopped at a cell door, hesitantly jingling the keys in his pocket. "Guess you better stay outside here and talk."

Slack Vincent's looks had not improved much. His eyes burned with a fearful desperation. "Thank God you got here, Grant. You know they're fixin' to hang me?" His hands trembled.

Caudell made no effort to cover his pent-up hatred. "I can't do anything about that. I just came for my money."

Vincent's bearded jaw fell. His bony hands gripped the steel bars. His eyes were wild as he stared into Caudell's face. "You'd just stand by and let them have me? My God, Grant, we was friends!"

"Friends? You shot me in the back and robbed me."

"I didn't *kill* you." The wildness gave way to a look of cunning, like a trapped wolf seeing a way out. "Sure I've got your money, Grant. And more besides. Luck's been runnin' with me, till today. But I ain't tellin' you where that money's at. Not as long as I'm in here. If you let them kill me, the secret dies too."

Anger ripped through Caudell, and he grabbed the bars. He realized his anger was futile. "What do you think I could do, Slack? I'm just one man. There must be a hundred out yonder waitin' to get their hands on you."

Slack Vincent wiped a dirty, ripped sleeve across his sweat-beaded forehead. "That's for you to figure out. It was you that figured how to get the cattle across the river when it was runnin' high. It was you that outsmarted them nesters and their quarantine line. So you get me out of here. Save me from that mob and I'll take you to your money. I stashed it away before I tried for this bank. It ain't far.

"Fail me, and it's good-bye to everything."

Grant Caudell stepped back, half sick to his stomach. He knew Slack Vincent meant business. The outlaw had all his chips in the game, and he was playing for his life.

In the outer office Caudell desperately faced the lawman. "Sheriff, can't you slip him out of here to someplace safe? You know you and those three deputies can't keep him long."

Wearily the sheriff threw up his hands. "We couldn't get him out of this jail without gettin' him shot. There's men watchin' out there from every side. If we was to make a run for it, chances are they'd shoot one or two of us as well.

"If there was any question he was guilty, I'd try it. But there ain't. If somebody has got to die tonight, it's goin' to be him, and nobody else."

Despairing, Grant Caudell looked through a barred window into the lamp-spotted darkness. He pictured Molly as he had kissed her good-bye that morning months ago, and as she had stood on the porch, lantern in her hand, watching him start his cattle herd north. Later she had traveled all the way in a wagon to be with him while he recuperated from the gunshot wound. She had tried to beg him off of Slack Vincent's trail, even though it meant losing their ranch, their home.

"You're a cowman, not a peace officer," she had argued.

But he had been desperate, for the ranch was likely to be the only big chance of their lives. If they lost it, he knew he would work for cow wages the rest of his life, and she would cook and scrub for hands. "I'll get our money back," he had declared, "or I'll put a marker on Slack Vincent's grave."

Now it looked as if he could start building that marker. He saw no answer.

Suddenly, he did. Upon the sheriff's desk lay Caudell's pistol, where one of the deputies had placed it. Caudell recoiled from his first impulse. But he considered, and he knew it was the only chance he had . . . the only chance Molly had.

He waited until a noise outside distracted the sheriff, then he picked up the pistol. The sheriff was looking through a rip in the window shade, trying to see what was happening down the street. Grant eased up behind him and poked him gently with the gun barrel.

"Don't make any noise. Just walk back into that corridor like nothin' was wrong."

The sheriff started to say something but choked it off. At the cell door Caudell took his gun. "Open that door, quick."

The lawman complied slowly, his face grave. "You're a fool. They'll cut you down when they see you come out with him."

Caudell did not answer. There was no answer to give.

Slack Vincent was out of the cell the instant the lock opened. A weak grin spread over his face. "I knowed that money would fetch you. Let me git a gun, and we'll ride out of here."

Grant shook his head. "One gun's enough. And *I'll* carry it."

He motioned the sheriff into the cell and closed the door behind him. "Sorry, Sheriff. I just can't see any other way."

The sheriff faced him grimly. "I don't know if you was tellin' me the truth or not, about him shootin' and robbin' you. If you wasn't, the hell with you. If you was, you better watch tight. He'll find a way to do it again."

Caudell tested the back door and found it locked. Glancing quickly over the sheriff's key ring, he found the key to fit it. Carefully he pulled the door open and looked outside. The back of the jail was unlighted, and he saw nothing. But he knew someone would be watching, out there in the pitch-black shadows.

He pointed. "My horse is over yonder. Let's run for it."

They jumped out the door abreast and struck a hard run toward the picket fence where he had tied his sorrel. Instantly someone shouted. A gun barked, and a bullet snarled overhead. Another shot followed, but the two men were quickly concealed in a black pool of darkness.

Caudell's horse shied as they ran up to him. Caudell grabbed the reins, rammed a foot into the stirrup and mounted. He reached for Slack and helped him swing up behind. Spurring out away from the excited shouting and the pounding of feet, Caudell kept a firm grip on the pistol in case Slack might try to grab it from his hand.

A horseman loomed up in front of them. Caudell sa
the man raise a gun. He spurred the sorrel and ramme
the man's horse. The rider's pistol exploded into the air ▪
he tumbled back out of the saddle.

Slack jumped down, grabbed the loose horse, an
mounted him. The two men bent low over their sadd
horns and spurred.

Pursuit was immediate. But the darkness of the bac
street worked in the fugitives' favor. Caudell and Vincer
hauled up quickly behind a building. A dozen riders whippe
by, shouting angrily, one or two tossing wild shots ahea
of them into the darkness.

Caudell realized suddenly that the building was a churcl
Catching his breath, he peered through the back windo
into a small room, then looked away. His conscience welle
up inside him like an accusing judge.

He had seen a gray-haired woman sitting in dry-eye
grief beside a long pine box, a handkerchief crushed in h▪
work-roughened hands.

For a moment Caudell considered calling the who
thing off and letting them have Slack Vincent. But years
hard work and desperate hope had gone into that rancl
that herd of cattle. At his age there would be no startir
over.

More riders spurred by. Watching their dim outline
as they passed in the darkness, Caudell murmured, "No\
whichaway's that money?"

Vincent pointed his narrow, bearded chin in the ger
eral direction the riders had taken. Caudell motioned wit
the pistol. "Move out, then. We'll follow along with ther
a ways and drop out. They won't be lookin' for us to b
amongst them."

A sudden thought struck him. He shook down his rop
and dropped a loop over Vincent's shoulders.

"What the hell?" Vincent exploded.

"Just to make sure you don't take a notion to get awa
from me in the dark. Try it and you'll break your neck."

Within a couple of miles the riders gave up the chase
"Have to wait for mornin'," Caudell could hear one of ther

say as the men and horses milled around. "We'll get us a couple of good trackers."

When the group turned toward town again, Caudell and Slack Vincent held back. Unnoticed in the darkness, they soon were alone in the scattering of brush. The hoofbeats rapidly faded away into the distance.

The long period of tension left Caudell weak for a time, his heart struggling. It required strong effort for him to keep up his guard, but he knew he must. To take his eyes from Vincent for even a moment might lead to losing him. "Let's be after what we came for," he said. "We can't afford to be here in the mornin' when they come back with somebody who can read tracks."

He made Vincent lead out. Caudell stayed close behind him, keeping the rope taut, for it would be easy for Vincent to slip the loop and spur away into the night.

For an hour they rode south and west, in as straight a line as the brushy terrain allowed. Whenever they ran into a thicket, Caudell made Vincent go around, though it meant extra distance. It would be too easy for Vincent to break loose and hide in in the brush.

Once Caudell caught Vincent taking up slack in the rope and attempting to slip it over his narrow shoulders.

Furious, Caudell jammed the muzzle of the pistol into Vincent's ribs so hard that the gaunt man grunted in pain. "Drop that rope before I blow a hole in you!"

Vincent hesitated, shrugged, then once more let the rope settle about his flat stomach. "You wouldn't kill me, Grant. You need me too bad."

Caudell gritted his teeth. "I'd cripple you. I'd do it with pleasure."

Presently they dropped into a brushy draw where the silted turf was soft and yielding to the horses' hoofs. On the ground Grant detected a sign of an old wagon trail that crossed over, one that wasn't used much anymore.

"Old road back to town," Vincent said. "We're almost there."

The shack came up unexpectedly out of darkness. Its rough, whipsawed siding was warped, badly split in places.

Most of the sections in the old glass windows had been broken, and the window frames had weathered out of shape. A night-feeding jackrabbit skittered away from the front door as the two horses plodded up.

"Don't look much like a bank, does it?" Vincent drawled.

Nervously Caudell motioned with the pistol. "Come on, come on. Let's find the money and get this over with."

Vincent stepped down. "All right if I take this rope off? Ain't like I was a horse that's got to be kept tied."

"All right, all right," Caudell nodded impatiently, looking for signs of first light in the eastern sky, though he knew it was still hours too early. "Hurry up."

After they had tied their horses, Vincent pushed open the sagging front door. Caudell was quick to follow him. He heard the crunch of rotten wood and felt the floor give way beneath his right foot. Falling to his knees, he forgot the pistol for a moment, then excitedly brought it back up to cover Vincent. In the scant light he saw Vincent take a quick step forward, then think better of it and stand back.

"Aimed to warn you about that hole," Vincent remarked. "Just slipped my mind."

Muttering, Caudell worked his foot loose and shakily stood up again, his hand tight on the pistol. "I'll bet it did. You got a lamp in here? If you have, light it."

Vincent grunted. "What if somebody was to spot it?"

"We'll take that chance. For all I know you could have a gun stashed in here. I want to be able to see."

Slack shrugged. "Trustin' soul, ain't you?"

Caudell heard the rattle of a lantern as Vincent slid it off a dusty shelf. Its smoky flame revealed a dirt-covered, disheveled shack with the beginnings of a pack-rat's nest in one corner. There was not even an old stove.

"The money," Caudell said sharply.

"Money!" Vincent replied. "I never saw anybody so hell-bent for money."

"It's not the money," Caudell said. "It's what it stands for. It's what I lose if I don't get it back." He did not expect Vincent to understand, and he wondered why he even tried to explain. He supposed he was trying to justify to himself what he had done, freeing a murderer who might murder again.

Slack Vincent hesitantly ran his tongue over his lips, plainly hating the thought of parting with the money. He carried the lamp over to the corner and shoved the rat's nest to one side with his boot. He knelt and pulled up loose boards. He lowered the lantern through the hole he had made in the floor.

"Might be a rattlesnake under there," he commented.

He brought up a lard bucket. Caudell's heart quickened.

"There's your money, Grant," Vincent said. "You been huntin' it for months. Now look at it."

Kneeling, Caudell nervously held the bucket with one hand and tried to push off the lid with the muzzle of the pistol. Glancing at Slack, wishing the man weren't so close, he laid the gun between his knees and put both hands to work on the tight lid. It sprang off and rolled across the floor with a sudden clatter.

Caudell looked inside the bucket, his whole body a-tingle. It was all there, from what he could see. All there—in his hands—after that long search, after all those sleepless, worrying nights.

He sensed a sudden movement. He jerked his head up just as Vincent hurled the lantern at his face. Caudell ducked and felt the missile bounce off his shoulder. Shouting something unintelligible, Vincent sprang after the lantern. He slammed his body into Caudell and sent him sprawling backward onto the rough floor.

"That's *my* money!" Vincent shrilled.

Caudell grunted at the crushing weight of the man's body. He lunged to one side and felt the weight shift. Vincent went out of balance. Caudell grabbed the man's collar and gave him a quick heave. Vincent went down.

They strugged on the floor. Caudell was vaguely aware that the flickering yellow flames had begun to feed on the dry wood where the lantern had spilled its kerosene. Somehow Caudell managed to get to his feet, swapping blows with Vincent.

A cold, silent fury drove at Caudell, a fury that had begun far away and long ago, that had steadily grown during a heartbreaking search across a long stretch of trail. It had swelled to a climax beside a little church, where he had seen a gray-haired woman sitting in anguish.

In blistering heat from the blazing shack, Caudell pounded his fists without mercy at Vincent's body. At last Vincent reeled senselessly out the door to stagger and fall on his face in the sand.

Only then did Caudell fully realize that the shack was ablaze around him, that his clothes were smouldering. His heart leaped in panic at the thought of that money going up in flames after all he had been through to retrieve it. He grabbed up the pistol and the bucket, oblivious to the heat that blistered his hands. He jumped out through the door, caught the half-conscious Vincent under the arm, and dragged him away.

While the fire still afforded light enough, he dumped the contents of the can and began to count. When he had figured off twenty-one thousand dollars, he rolled it and put it into his saddlebags. The rest he shoved into Vincent's pockets.

Vincent stirred. Caudell cut a short piece off of his rope and roughly bound the man's wrists.

Vincent pleaded, "That's too tight. It's cuttin' me."

Caudell's face was clouded. "Shut up and be glad it isn't your throat. Now get back on your horse."

Vincent staggered to his feet and wavered uncertainly. Caudell prodded him with the pistol. "Get on." He tied the man's thin wrists securely to the saddle horn.

Vincent queried fearfully, "Grant, what you fixin' to do?"

Caudell stared at him without mercy. "You know, Slack, for a little while there I had a crazy notion about lettin' you go. But not now. I'm takin' you back to town."

Suddenly Slack Vincent was trembling. "No, Grant, you promised!"

"I promised nothin'. And if I had, the promise would've been off after you tried to jump me."

Leading Vincent's horse, he found the faded wagon trail and followed its meandering course northeastward.

The town was quiet as they returned. A dim promise of dawn was beginning to show in the east. Here and there a lamp sent its weak yellow light against the darkness. Caudell noted a dim glow in the jail windows as he rode up behind the building and dismounted. He tied the reins of Slack's mount to a fence.

"Listen to me, Grant," Vincent pleaded. "You can take my money too, all of it, if you'll cut this rope off of me."

Caudell shook his head. "I'm takin' just what's comin' to me, Slack. And you'll take what's comin' to *you*.

"Maybe the lynchin' fever's burned out by now. Things generally look different in the daylight. You can use your money to hire you a lawyer, if you think it'll do you any good. I doubt that it will. Adios, Slack."

Slack Vincent's jaw dropped. He was almost crying. "Grant, for God's sake—"

Caudell drew his pistol and fired three times into the air. He held back his fidgety horse until he heard a shout and the quick strike of boots upon the jailhouse floor.

Then he reined the horse around and spurred him out into the darkness.

Lonesome Ride to Pecos

Cautiously watching the dust settle, Deputy Sheriff Andy Hayes holstered his smoking six-shooter and walked to the fallen and dying man. The young robber stared up at him with wide and frightened eyes. One hand over the growing red splotch on his chest, the gasping outlaw turned his head toward the little plume of hoof-churned dust that hid his escaping partner. His lips moved, but only a groan came. In a moment Hayes forced himself to kneel and close the sightless eyes.

He shuddered in revulsion for what he had had to do. He would not sleep tonight. Wishing he were somewhere else, doing anything else in the world for a living, he reluctantly searched the robber's pockets for identification. It was a bitter thing to kill a man, leaving a scar that he knew would always be with him. It was even more bitter because the man had been so young, by the look of him probably an impatient cowboy wanting to make his stake in one day.

Hayes found a letter inside the worn vest. Finished but never sealed, it was addressed to Pecos and signed *Tommy Clyde*.

The deputy's big hands trembled as he read what the cowboy had written to a girl named Julie, pouring out his love, telling her he was on a cattle trade which would stock their little ranch and give them the start for which they had waited.

Hayes found himself visualizing the girl named Julie. He saw her—painfully—in the image of another whose

57

name had been Mary, disapproving of guns and men who wore them, marrying a young minister who, like her, would never have use for them.

He heard running horses, and he slipped the letter into his shirt pocket. Placing the cowboy's dusty hat over the still face, he pushed to his feet. He blinked stinging eyes as the possemen reined up in a swirl of dust.

A grim-faced Elton McReady gave the dead man a glance that was without compassion. He said to Hayes, "Killed one, I see. Did you get the money back?"

Hayes raked a quick glance over the riders. Reluctantly he brought his gaze back to McReady, trying not to react to the man's eternal baiting. "His partner must've been carryin' it. He's took to the tall brush."

McReady bit hard on the dead cigar clamped between his teeth. "Then you ought to've killed *him* too."

Hayes's face warmed. "One dead man ought to be enough."

"Not when the other has got the bank's money." He pointed in the direction in which the survivor had fled. "How come you to stop here? Why didn't you keep on after him?"

Someday, Hayes promised himself, he was going to mash that cigar across McReady's face. "My horse is wounded."

"You could've caught this man's and kept on goin'."

Hayes said, "Yes, I could've. But I didn't. You go on after him if you've a mind to. His horse is faster, so you won't catch him, any more than I would've. But you can make a chase out of it, and maybe you'll feel like you've done your do."

McReady said gruffly, "I reckon I'll just do that." He glanced around him. "Come on, boys, let's get after him."

Hayes found a friendly face and beckoned with his chin. "March, would you mind goin' back to town and fetchin' a wagon?" The rest of the posse spurred out. Hayes watched them, knowing they would drag back after a while, exhausted and empty-handed. Not a horse in the bunch could catch the fast bay the second outlaw had been riding.

Hayes turned his back on them and saw after his own

horse, standing braced in mute agony, head down. Hayes gathered his strength, unsaddled, drew his pistol and fired.

A couple of hours later old Sheriff Tol Murphy limped to the wagon in the street and lifted the tarp to look. He muttered bitterly about waste and gently let the tarp settle back into place. "The pity is that he died for so damned little," he said. "The teller kept his wits about him and didn't give them nothin' but blank checks and bills of low denomination. They didn't get more than three hundred dollars. Not near enough to die for."

Hayes asked himself silently, *How much is enough to die for?* He said, "It could be enough to leave *us* in bad shape, though, me and you. McReady'll see to that."

The sheriff did not seem to have considered McReady. He shrugged, indicating he could do nothing anyway.

Hayes told him McReady had led the posse on what was sure to be a futile chase. "He'll make the effort look good, at least, to help him run against you in the summer election."

Murphy nodded, his eyes sad. "I hope you know another trade, son. You may not have this one after the vote's counted." He stared at the wagon, his mind returning dutifully to the more immediate problem. "Any idea who he is?"

Hayes took the letter from his pocket. Murphy held it to arm's length but had to carry it back into the office and get his glasses. Sitting at his desk, he mulled over the letter in silence a long time. "Nothin' said here about his partner. Think you'd know him if you saw him?"

Hayes shook his head. "Not to hold water in court."

The sheriff read the letter one more time. "Then I think it'd be a good idea if you went out to Pecos. Don't tell anybody a damned thing. Just find an excuse to hang around there and watch. Maybe you'll get lucky." The frown returned. "If you don't, ain't much use you comin' back. I'll probably be swampin' out old Emery's stable for a livin'."

The county furnished Hayes a new horse, a long-legged sorrel that reached out and gathered in the miles with an easy trot that carried him halfway across West Texas in less time than Hayes expected . . . less time than he wanted. He was in no hurry, for he dreaded Pecos. He toyed with a temptation to send back a written resignation and payment for the sorrel. He might have done it had he not felt an obligation to Murphy.

He crossed the Conchos, then rode westward across the dry desert country, following a wagon road that set him a crooked path through stunted mesquite and greasewood country. In Pecos City a saloonkeeper gave him directions to the Slash C. "If I was lookin' for a job, that sure wouldn't be my choice of the place to go. One of these days they're goin' to have a contest to find the sorriest ranch in Reeves County. That one and about three more will tie for first place."

"A job's a job."

"Well, come the end of the month, be sure they pay you in cash money. Don't take no promises."

Hayes sat on the edge of a hill west of the narrow river. He stared down toward two wooden windmill towers, a little cluster of corrals, and a few small frame buildings at the edge of a scrub-brush draw. Between him and the ranch headquarters stretched a broad and nearly barren alkali flat. If this place tied for first prize, he thought, he would not care to see the others. He had hardly seen even a jackrabbit the last two or three miles. He could understand why.

Then he saw the girl sitting on the edge of a narrow porch at the front of a small box-and-strip house. She was tiny, hair light brown, done up in a bun on the back of her head. Not until he was near enough to speak to her could he see that she held a kitten in her lap, gently washing its eyes with milk. She looked up. Her face was not that of the girl named Mary after all, but it did not matter. Mary's image faded from his mind. It was as if this face was the one he had been seeing all the time. A pretty face, to be sure, but it brought him a chill. This had to be the Julie of the letter.

He forced a thin smile. "Kind of fudgin' on Nature, ain't you? That kitten may not be *ready* to see yet." Three more were in a squirming mass beside her.

She said, "The world won't be any prettier for puttin' it off." He sensed a bitter edge in her voice.

He said, "I was told in town that I might find a job here. They said you-all had . . . lost a man."

She looked at the ground, so he could not see her eyes. "The owner's son . . . outlaws killed him."

Outlaws. Well, he thought, that was as good a story as any, if the family wanted to spare a wayward boy's memory.

The girl stroked the kitten a moment before she trusted herself to look up again at Hayes. She said, "Maybe if you'd talk to Mr. Clyde . . ." She looked toward the brush corrals.

Hayes saw the outline of a man beyond a fence built of mesquite branches stacked between double rows of heavy posts. The man did not seem to be moving. Throat tight in sympathy, Hayes touched the sagging brim of his hat and led the sorrel toward the corrals.

A rifle shot stopped him. He reached instinctively for his pistol as the horse jumped back in fright. He saw a movement at the edge of the alkali flat. A coyote ran a few steps, fell, threshed a moment and went still. Shaky, Hayes slipped the pistol back into its holster and walked to the fence. A short, stocky man hobbled toward him on the opposite side. "Hope I didn't give you a fright," the ranchman said. "Damned coyote comes after the chickens every time we turn our backs." He tried to meet Hayes's gaze but could not hold it. His eyes seemed haunted.

Hayes gave him time to collect himself. "I heard in town you might be lookin' to hire a hand."

The rancher was probably not so old as he looked at this moment. "Bad news travels fast, don't it?"

Hayes was not sure how to answer. "Always seems like."

The rancher looked again toward the coyote, hiding his eyes as the girl had done. "They tell you about my boy?"

Hayes thought about his answer. "Said he had been killed, was all."

Hatred crept into the man's voice. "Someday maybe I'll face the man that done it. I'll shoot him with no more compunctions than I shot that coyote." His eyes showed a moment of fire. When that burned away, a bleakness remained. He looked Hayes up and down, making a quick judgment. "Amos Worth is the foreman. Go tell him I've hired you."

He turned away, then back. "That shack yonder is the closest thing we've got to a bunkhouse. You'll be the only hand in it till Duff Daggett gets back."

Hayes swung into the saddle and rode to the bunkhouse to throw his bag and roll of blankets onto an empty steel cot. Someone stepped into the doorway, blocking much of the light. Cautiously, thinking of the second robber, Hayes turned. He saw a tall, gaunt man almost as old as Clyde, wearing the weathered, dried-out look of a man who seldom let daylight catch him under a roof.

"I'm Amos Worth," the man said, withholding welcome until sure of Hayes's business there.

Hayes said, "Mr. Clyde told me to hunt you up. I just hired on."

Worth extended his hand. "We can use the help. But you've come at a sad time."

"So I gather." Hayes did not want to ask too many questions, but he already harbored a suspicion. "Mr. Clyde told me there's supposed to be another hand here."

"Duff Daggett. Him and Tommy Clyde left a while back to buy some cattle on the Llano. We got a message from him that robbers killed Tommy. Duff taken a bullet himself, but he sent word he'll be back soon's he's able to ride."

Guardedly, Hayes asked, "Where did this happen?"

"Duff's letter didn't say. Old John's sent messages to every sheriff in two hundred miles, tryin' to find out."

The foreman's eyes showed no sign he was covering up the facts. Hayes concluded that Worth was telling the truth as he knew it. Sheriff Tol Murphy had evidently sent no word to John Clyde. He was leaving Hayes a chance to work things out in his own time.

Hayes fingered the badge, hidden in his pocket, and wondered if he—or somebody—had actually hit Duff Daggett as he was getting away from the bank. One dead, one wounded, for less than three hundred dollars.

He asked, "That girl . . . is she Mr. Clyde's daughter?"

"Not his, *mine*. Tommy Clyde had it in his mind to marry her soon's he got the land John was fixin' to give him."

Hayes's eyes narrowed. "Then *you* lost a son too, in a manner of speakin'."

Worth nodded grimly. "I ain't sure Julie was as set on it as Tommy was. The boy had his rough spots, but I felt like he'd've made my girl happy."

From the only window in the little shack, Hayes could see the girl in a chicken yard back of her house, feeding grain to a wing-flapping cluster of brownish hens. Wind tugged at the full skirt of an old gray cotton dress, but it barely lifted the hem as high as her ankles. It was not possible, he thought, that he could be in love with a girl he had met only once. But he had been seeing her in his mind since he had first read that letter.

Careful, Hayes, he told himself. *She'll hate you when she finds out. And she'll have to find out.*

Duff Daggett had been the second man in the bank. Of that Hayes was already convinced. The teller would make the identification easily. All Hayes had to do was stay here and wait for Daggett to come back.

He had cowboyed for years before he had gone to work for the county, but he did not remember that the work had ever been as hard as following old John Clyde. The rancher was a furious engine of a man, pushing himself and Hayes and Amos Worth at a back-breaking pace from daylight until dark.

Once when the old man loped his horse out of hearing to push some shaded-up cattle from a brushy draw, Hayes observed, "He must be drivin' himself to help him through his grief."

Worth shook his head. "No, fact is he's slacked off some. You ought to've seen how he used to work . . . . before."

Hayes frowned. "Maybe he drove the boy too hard." He had been about to say *drove the boy to what he did*. That might have spilled the whole story.

"A man has to be hard and tough to make it on the

Pecos River," Worth said. "Somebody called the Pecos the grave of a cowman's hopes. John just does what the country demands of him."

Despite the grueling pace, Hayes came to respect John Clyde and Amos Worth. The harsh days were tempered by his anticipation of seeing Julie in the evening. Around sunset each day he would ride a weary horse into the big corral with Amos and the brooding John Clyde, his nerves tight with dread that this would be the day Duff Daggett had come back, that this would be the time all facts must be revealed and the acceptance he had earned from these people would turn to hatred.

Julie had begun to smile, sometimes. Hayes avoided telling her anything that would make her realize he was or ever had been a lawman, but he told her stories of his upbringing on the San Saba, of hunting wildcats and wolves, of falling into the river while trying to retrieve a big catfish, of horses that he had broken and that had come near breaking him. The stories often brought light to her eyes and crowded out the grief he so hated to see there.

Evenings, sometimes, he milked the cow for her, something he had not done since he had left the family homeplace. Because she was the only woman in the foreman's house, it was expected of her that she cook for whatever single men were on the ranch, which at this time meant her widowed father, Clyde, and Hayes. Hayes took it for granted that Clyde's wife was dead, but Amos told him she was not. She had decided years ago that life on a Pecos River ranch was too hard for her, and she had gone to El Paso, leaving her husband and son behind.

Often Hayes followed Julie into the kitchen after supper and dried the dishes as she washed them. Watching her, he knew he did not want to live the rest of his life a bachelor. He told himself it was reckless to let this girl arouse these feelings in him, for it was inevitable that the warmth he saw more and more in her eyes would turn one day soon to contempt.

But one night, as he gazed at her, he let a wet cup slip out of his hand and fall to the floor with a clatter. Both reached for it, and their hands met. For a moment he clutched her fingers, not wanting to turn loose, and she made no effort to pull away. He tried for words that would not come. Color flushed her cheeks, and then she was in his arms. He told her without words what he had wanted to say from the beginning.

He went to the bunkhouse in a black mood, wishing he had never come here. He lay awake a long time, torn. At one point he went to the barn, intending to saddle the sorrel horse and ride away, to avoid the black day that must come.

Any other night the horse would have been there, staying close for the morning's welcome bait of oats. This night he had strayed off into the pasture, far out in the darkness. Hayes went back to the bunkhouse, his resolve weakening. By morning, when he saw Julie again, he knew he could not leave her that way, at least not yet a while.

By night it was too late. Duff Daggett came back.

He was standing beside the little saddle shed when Hayes and Amos Worth rode in that evening. At some other time, in some other place, Hayes would not have recognized him. But here, he could be no one else. Walking out to meet Amos, Daggett carried himself stiffly. He had not lied about being wounded, only about the circumstances under which it had happened. Somehow, Hayes was disappointed. He had pictured Daggett as some callous outlaw, riding away with the spoils, coldly leaving his partner to die. But Hayes saw here a guileless face, a cowboy as young as the one who had died.

Daggett stared at Hayes with suspicion, even after Amos explained how Hayes came to be there. Amos placed his hand on Daggett's shoulder, and Hayes sensed the old foreman's fondness for the youth. "You been over to tell John how it happened?"

Daggett nodded grimly. "Hardest thing ever I done, Amos. Made me wish it had been me instead of Tommy."

Amos said sympathetically, "I imagine you done all a man could, under the circumstances. Old John's been tryin' for a month to find out where his boy is buried. You tell him?"

Daggett replied, "I told him. Now he wants me to take

him and fetch Tommy's body home." He glanced at Amos in apprehension. "I wisht you'd talk him out of the notion."

"The boy belongs here, buried at home."

Daggett argued weakly, "It'll be an ordeal for the old man."

"He's already been through his worst ordeal. Maybe this would give him peace."

Daggett seemed unconvinced. He looked to Hayes as if for help, as if forgetting he was a stranger. A little suspicion came back into his eyes. "Ain't I met you somewhere?"

Hayes's heart made a little jump. It stood to reason that Daggett and Tommy Clyde had spent time in town before the robbery, looking over the layout. Daggett might have noticed him then because of his badge. Hayes tried to bar the worry from his eyes. "You ever been in the San Saba country?" he asked.

"No," Daggett said. "You must just look like somebody."

"Poor feller," Hayes replied, "whoever he is."

Daggett turned his attention back to Amos Worth. "I wisht you'd talk to John. I don't want to go back there. I just *can't* look at the place again where it happened."

Amos again placed his hand on the cowboy's shoulder. "I wouldn't ask you to go through a thing like this for *me*. But this is for *him*. You don't know what he's been through."

"I *do* know, Amos. I been through it too." Tears brimmed in Daggett's eyes.

Hayes turned away. Because of John Clyde and Julie, he had known this would be a hard thing to do. He had not considered that it would be hard because of Daggett too.

Supper was somber and quiet, nobody wanting to talk. Hayes watched Julie, wishing he could tell her, knowing he couldn't.

Sleep was out of the question. He lay staring into the darkness, again considering the possibility of simply riding away from there, of writing Tol Murphy a letter saying the trail had gone cold. Even as he pondered that option, he knew it was something he could not do.

Upwards of midnight he heard the gentle creaking of a steel cot as Duff Daggett swung his legs over the side. Hayes turned his head slowly and watched Daggett quietly putting on his clothes, stuffing his few belongings into a canvas bag, rolling up his blankets. Barefoot, Daggett carried the things outside and paused on the moonlit step to pull on his boots.

Hayes quickly dressed, then brought his six-shooter from its hiding place beneath his pillow. He eased the door shut and made his way from one dark patch of shadow to another until he reached the corral. Duff Daggett awkwardly swung his saddle up onto a horse's back, his stiff arm limiting his movement.

Hayes said, "You'd just as well slip that saddle off. You ain't goin' anywhere till daylight."

Daggett whirled, eyes widening as he saw the pistol in Hayes's hand. He tried to speak, but the words seemed to catch in his mouth. He reached up with his good hand and gripped the arm that had taken the wound. Finally he managed to ask, "You some kind of law?"

Hayes nodded. "You owe a debt back there where you-all robbed that bank. Looks to me like you owe a debt to that old man too. You was fixin' to run out on both of them."

Daggett seemed about to buckle at the knees. He leaned against his horse for support. "You the one that put a bullet in my arm?"

Hayes nodded. "Probably. I didn't know I'd done it."

"Then you'd be the one that shot Tommy too."

Hayes felt his throat tighten. "I wish I could say otherwise. I've wished a thousand times. . . ."

"So have I. I ain't had a minute's rest since it happened."

"Where's the money, Daggett?"

"Never was much of it to start with. What I didn't spend for the doctorin' I've still got in my bag. I swear to God, I'll send them the rest of it soon's I can find me another

67

job. Just let me get away from here so I don't have to tell John."

Hayes said with regret, "I can't do that. If I could, I'd do it for myself."

"Then if you've got to take me back, do it now, tonight, while he's asleep."

"No, Daggett. We've *both* got to face him. We'll wait till daylight."

Daggett looked up at the position of the Big Dipper. "Goin' to be a long night."

"There's already *been* a lot of long nights."

Hayes walked him back to the little bunkhouse. "You'd just as well lay down," he said. "*One* of us ought to get some rest." Daggett would be easier to watch, lying on his back. Hayes lighted the lamp and sat in a rawhide-bottomed chair to wait the night through. He heard every nightbird that called in the darkness, every howl of a coyote far down toward the Pecos. His eyes burned, and his eyelids were heavy.

Daggett lay still most of the time, but Hayes knew he did not sleep. Once he asked, "What do you think they'll do to me?"

"There wasn't any citizen killed, or even hurt. We'll be takin' part of the money back. If you behave yourself, maybe they won't give you too long a sentence."

Miserably Daggett said, "I've got a *life* sentence ahead of me, just rememberin' what happened."

Hayes had no comfort to offer him.

Daylight seemed three nights in coming. At last Hayes saw the rose glow of dawn breaking through the window. Lamplight was yellow in the kitchen of the Worth house. He pushed to his feet and found his legs stiff, reluctant to move. "We'd better be gettin' it done," he said.

He kept the pistol in his hand, but he did not point it directly at Daggett. He had a feeling he would not need to fire it. He let Daggett walk ahead of him.

Julie had a smile for them as they came through the door. "Mornin', both of you." The smile died as she saw the pistol.

"Julie," Hayes said, "I wish you'd fetch Mr. Clyde over here. Duff Daggett and me have got somethin' to tell him."

Amos Worth came through the door of his tiny bedroom, stuffing his shirttail into his trousers. He stared at the pistol but asked no questions. Hayes had an idea from the dismay in his face that he was already sensing the truth. He watched his daughter hurry out the door, then said, "If you boys got anything to tell me before John gets here . . ."

Hayes said, "Be ready to help him. He'll need a friend."

Tears were in Daggett's eyes again.

John Clyde stopped in the doorway and stared wide-eyed at the two young men, at Hayes's pistol pointed vaguely toward the ceiling. Julie came in behind him and stood at his side. Hayes said, "Mr. Clyde, you'd better sit down. This boy has got somethin' to tell you."

Clyde stepped toward Daggett, but Hayes motioned him back. "I'd rather you stood clear of him." He fished the badge from his pocket and showed it, then put it back. John Clyde seated himself heavily in a straight chair, his shoulders drooped. Like Amos, he seemed to sense some of what was coming.

In a broken voice Daggett explained. "It didn't happen like I told you, Mr. Clyde. Me and Tommy went to buy them cattle, but we didn't know the market had taken a big jump. We didn't have near enough money for what Tommy wanted to buy. We seen a high-stakes poker game in a dramshop over there, and the players acted like a bunch of amateurs. Tommy taken a notion he could run up that bankroll and get his cattle after all.

"They wasn't the amateurs; *we* was. That roll didn't last no time, hardly, and Tommy was broke. He was scared to come back to you and Julie and own up to what he'd done. Well, there was this little crackerbox bank. We taken a notion it'd be easy pickin's, but it wasn't. One of them lawmen killed Tommy and put a bullet in my arm. I thought I'd got away, till last night." He glanced at Hayes, then looked at the floor.

Hayes reached in his shirt pocket. "Julie, this is for you." He gave her the letter from Tommy Clyde.

Her hands trembled as she realized what it was. Tears came, and she could not read it. "How did you come to have this?"

"I found it in Tommy Clyde's pocket, after . . ." He swallowed. "I'm sorry, Julie. I wish it'd been different."

John Clyde sat with head bowed, shoulders shaking. "Scared to come and tell me. I thought I'd raised my boy not to be scared of anything. I reckon I made him scared of *me*." After a time he lifted his burning eyes to Hayes. "He said a lawman killed my boy. Are you that man?"

Hayes forced himself to hold his gaze to those terrible eyes. "Yes, sir. I am."

John Clyde pushed to his feet and staggered across the little room, apparently without aim or purpose except to give his emotions an outlet in movement instead of in a cry. But he had purpose. Too late to stop him, Hayes saw the rifle standing in a corner. Clyde grabbed it and spun around, swinging the muzzle toward Hayes. He cocked back the hammer.

Julie cried out in fear. Amos shouted, "John, don't . . ."

Hayes's stomach went cold. His hand seemed paralyzed on the pistol. He had killed *one* Clyde.

Duff Daggett jumped from his chair and threw himself between the old man and Hayes. "No, Mr. Clyde! Me and Tommy made a bad-enough mistake. Don't you make another."

"Out of my way, Duff," Clyde shouted, trying to shove past him.

Daggett grabbed the barrel and pushed it upward. The blast shook the thin walls. For a moment everyone seemed frozen. Then Daggett sighed and sank slowly to his knees.

John Clyde dropped the rifle and grabbed the sagging cowboy. "My God!" he rasped, "I didn't go to shoot you." Holding to Duff, he looked up pleadingly. "Somebody help!"

Hayes took two long strides, picked up the rifle and threw it out the door. Then he knelt beside Duff Daggett, whose face was graying like clay as shock set in. John Clyde was tearing desperately at Daggett's shirt. "Duff! Boy! I didn't go to do it!"

Hayes said, "Bullet went up through his shoulder. Same arm that was hit before."

The wound bled badly, but the slug had gone through. Julie rushed out of the room and appeared again with some cloths. Hayes said, "If we can just stop the blood . . ."

"Damn fool kid," Amos Worth gritted. "But his heart is in the right place."

John Clyde made his way back to his chair and sat down, silent, shattered, while Hayes and Amos and Julie worked on Daggett. They stopped the blood, soaked the wound with kerosene, then wrapped it. Amos said, "I'll bring the wagon around. John, me and you better haul him to town." Clyde nodded. His eyes were closed, tears on his face.

Julie's eyes pleaded with Hayes. "What'll you do to him?"

"Nothin', for now," Hayes said. "I couldn't take him back, the shape he's in. Maybe they'll take into account the price he's already paid. It's a chance anyway."

John Clyde stared at Hayes, and Hayes knew Clyde could never entirely forgive. It was too much to expect of him. Clyde said, "Whatever the bank is short, I'll make it up. This good boy won't be left beholden. My boy either." He paused, trying not to cry. "But don't come back for it. I'll send it. Better for both of us if we don't set eyes on one another again."

Amos brought the wagon up to the door. Julie spread blankets in the wagonbed, and the men carefully placed Daggett on them. Amos climbed back onto the seat. John Clyde knelt beside the cowboy. He was saying quietly, "You rest easy, son. Ain't nobody goin' to hurt you again as long as I'm here to do somethin' about it." The wagon started out upon the town road, Amos clucking the team into a brisk trot.

Hayes walked to the bunkhouse and gathered his few belongings, then went to the barn and saddled the sorrel horse.

Julie stayed at the house, watching him. He rode back to her and dismounted, struggling for the words to keep him from losing her. "I reckon this changes everything between us."

She said, "You'll have to give me time."

He swallowed. "How'll I know when it's been time enough?"

She tried to smile but could not quite make it work. "You'll know. I'll come lookin' for you."

"I won't be hard to find." He swung into the saddle. When he looked back, she was still watching. She waved, and some of the weight of the past weeks lifted from his shoulders. He knew someday he would look around, and she would be there.

Coward

His hands tense on the leather lines, Dick Fladness flicked a quick, searching glance at the two women who shared the tight buckboard seat with him.

"Brownwood just ahead," he said.

He might as well have said nothing, for the women sat in dusty, tight-lipped silence, their eyes brittle on the scattering of frame buildings that spread out across the open prairie west of Pecan Bayou.

Dick's mouth went hard again, and he flipped the reins at the ill-matched team to pick them up a little. He had hoped the long, hot ride might wear down the contempt that stood like an adobe wall between the women and himself. It had not.

He turned the corner by the blacksmith shop, and the trailing dust from the buckboard wheels caught up with him for a moment. Nora Matson sneezed. It was the first sound the girl had made the whole way in, except that she had sobbed quietly when they first pulled away from the stark pile of gray ashes and charred wood that had been the Matson ranch home.

Dick pulled up in front of the hotel on Center Street and climbed down, wrapping the reins around the right front wheel. He held up his callused hands to help Nora's mother down from the buckboard. Her eyes lashed him in scorn. She was a tall, graying woman with a stiff puritan pride.

"I can get down by myself."

Her daughter followed her. Nora was eighteen, slender

73

and pretty, with wide brown eyes that used to dance in laughter. Nora's eyes never touched Dick's face now, not while he was looking.

"I'll bring in your things," he said, nodding toward the small bundle of clothing under the buckboard seat.

Mrs. Matson cut him short. "We can manage that too. There's not much of it, since the fire."

Wincing, Dick stood silently by the buckboard wheel while the two women climbed the steps to the high plank gallery of the frame hotel. The balding proprietor hurried out and took the bundle from Nora Matson's hands. He turned solemnly around to the girl's mother.

"We heard about your son, Mrs. Matson. I'm terribly sorry."

She acknowledged his sympathy with a quick nod of her chin, which suddenly was set harder than ever. Stiffly she went on into the hotel, Nora behind her. The hotel man paused for a quick glance at Dick. His frown showed that he knew. The whole town must know.

Head down, Dick stepped up into the buckboard and flipped the reins. He pulled the team back around and rolled down to the livery barn at the end of the dusty street. He was conscious of idle eyes following him. He drew up within and tried to convince himself that he didn't care.

Mike Lavender walked out through the big open door of the frame livery barn and waited for him. Mike was a stiffened old cowhand who had had to seek an easier way to round out his days. His leather-dry face was expressionless, but Dick felt a quiet friendliness in the faded blue eyes. He leaned eagerly toward that friendliness, needing it for strength.

"Walter Matson's buckboard and team, Mike," Dick spoke. "Walter said let you take care of them."

Dick took his war bag and bedroll from the buckboard and started out. He walked with a faint limp.

Mike Lavender's eyes followed him. "What about you, Dick? What you goin' to do?"

Dick stopped in the open doorway, his saddle slung

over his shoulder. "Leave, I reckon. Go someplace where people haven't heard of me. Then maybe I can start over."

Mike Lavender shook his head. "You can't run away from a thing like this, Dick. It'll follow you. Take my advice and stay right here."

Dick dropped the saddle heavily, desperation raising the color in his face. "Look, Mike, I'm a coward. Anybody'll tell you. I lost my head in a fight, turned tail and deserted my friends. And a man died."

He lifted his hands. "Mike, do you think I could stay here and have people lookin' at me the way they will, like I was a coyote or somethin'? Snickerin' at me, maybe callin' me a coward to my face?"

Mike's pale eyes were patient. "Talk's cheap. You don't have to listen to it." The old cowpuncher's voice softened. "Son, these things have got a way of workin' themselves out if you just give them a chance. Now, you pitch your bedroll on that spare cot back yonder. You're stayin' with me for a spell."

Dick stood uncertainly, weighing Mike's words. It was going to be tough, staying here with the name the town would give him. But it would be tougher leaving, for the memory would be with him always, haunting him with the image of what might have been, the futile knowledge of things left undone.

If he left now, there would never be any coming back. He thought of Nora Matson, the tinkling music of her voice, the warmth of her cheek against his as they stood in the moonlight, the cool evening breeze searching leisurely across the bayou.

Leave, and anything there might have been between them would be finished. Maybe if . . .

He picked up the bedroll and carried it to the empty cot.

Mike slouched in a cane-bottomed chair, idly whittling a stick of kindling wood down to a sliver. His pale eyes lifted as Dick came back. He said, "I've heard the story the way it's been told around town. I'd like to hear it your way."

Squatting on the ground, Dick stared hollowly at the pile of pine shavings growing around Mike's big, worn-out boots.

"You've probably heard it just the way it happened," he said. "It's the barbed-wire fences that caused it. Ansel Hornby and his free-grassers have been cuttin' Walter Matson's fence, and we've been patchin' it right up again. Three nights ago they cut it and left a placard hangin' on a fencepost. Said if the fence went back up they would end the fight once and for all. Walter tore up the placard, and we fixed the fence.

"They waited till the sheriff had to be out of the country. Then last night they came. They were masked, but I know Ansel Hornby was leadin' them. And I recognized the voice of Branch Collin, that foreman of his. They didn't stop at the fence. They came right on to the house. We were puttin' up a good fight, Walter and his son Lindy and three of us hands. Then they somehow set fire to the house."

Dick's hands began to tremble. "I tried, Mike. I tried to stay there and fight. But those flames got to reachin' at me. My clothes went to smokin'. I couldn't stand it. I jumped out the door and broke to runnin'. All I could think of was to get away from that fire. I didn't quit runnin' till I fell. I laid there till I finally got a grip on myself. I could tell the shootin' had stopped. The fence cutters were gone. The house was gone. And Lindy Matson was dead."

Dick's head was in his hands. "Wasn't a one of them would speak to me. They all looked at me like I had killed Lindy myself. Came daylight, the cowboys rode after some neighbor help. Everybody went up on the hill to bury Lindy. They wouldn't let me help carry him. They wouldn't even let me help dig his grave.

"And when it was all over, Walter told me to go. I brought the women to town, where they'll be safe. Walter stayed. Swore he was goin' to put the fence back up and fight Hornby's free-grass men till he's dead." His face was grim. "He meant it, Mike. He's got the guts of a Mexican bull. But Hornby'll kill him. He knows the county's watchin' Walter. He knows if Walter's fence stays up, there'll be others, and the free-grass men will be fenced out. He won't quit till Walter's dead."

Sitting on the edge of his cot, trying to figure out what to do, Dick heard the clatter of horses' hoofs coming up from behind the barn. He caught the unintelligible conversation and the lift of careless laughter. Dick glanced at Mike and saw that the old cowboy was bent over in an uneasy nap.

Dick arose and walked toward the front of the barn. The limp was momentarily heavy from his having sat awhile. He heard riders hauling up on their reins and swinging to the ground in a jingling of spurs.

"Hey, Lavender," a rough voice called, "how about us throwin' our horses in a corral here for a while?"

Dick's heartbeat quickened. That voice belonged to Branch Collin. Dick hesitated, looking back at the sleeping Mike Lavender. Then he walked on to the door. Facing Collin, he jerked a thumb toward Lavender's pens.

"Mike's asleep, but I reckon it's all right."

Branch Collin was a medium-tall, slender man with a quick, easy movement and a sharp, sensitive face. There was a hint of green in his eyes that seemed always to contain a devilish laughter. Ansel Hornby was boss of the ranch, but Branch Collin was undisputed boss when it came to trouble. There were people two counties away who broke into a cold sweat at the mention of his name.

Collin seemed momentarily surprised at sight of Dick. Then the laughter came to his eyes. "Richard the Lion-Hearted. I reckon you found where you really belong, swampin' a stable."

Dick gritted his teeth and held his anger inside.

Ansel Hornby kneed a big roan horse up closer. He had a narrow, intense face. Dick had never seen him smile. Hornby's voice was flat and grim. "Boy, you should never have quit runnin'. You should have kept goin' till you were clear out of the country. I would advise you to move on now."

Anger beat against Dick, but his throat was tight. He could not speak.

Branch Collin said, "He'll leave, Ansel." Collin's smile lingered. His eyes dwelt heavily on Dick's. "But not before he puts up our horses for us."

Dick opened the gate for the men to ride in. There were five besides Hornby and Collin. They unsaddled and turned their horses loose in the corral.

Collin shook his finger under Dick's nose. "You feed them horses good, you hear? Otherwise you'll find yourself runnin' faster than you did last night."

A couple of the men chuckled. Enjoying the approval of the little audience, Collin suddenly pulled Dick's hat down over his eyes, hard. "There, that's just to be sure your hat don't blow off while you're runnin'."

Trembling with anger and humiliation, Dick pulled his hat up. Collin and the men were walking away, laughing. But Ansel Hornby stood there, his humorless eyes on Dick's blazing face.

"Man down the road said you brought the Matson women in. They put up at the hotel?"

Dick's answer came brittle and sharp. "You leave the women alone!"

Hornby's eyes widened in speculation at this unexpected hardness in the cowboy who had run away. "I'm not here to hurt the women. But sometimes you can reason with a woman when you can't talk to her men." His eyes narrowed again. "You had better consider what I told you, Fladness. You can ride a good way between now and dark."

Hornby turned and broke into a brisk stride to catch up with his men. Their spurred boots raised puffs of dry dust in the street. Dick watched Hornby point toward the hotel. But Collin shook his head and jerked his thumb at the saloon. Pleasure before business.

Dick's mind turned to Nora Matson and her mother. If only Sheriff Adams were in town. . . .

Dick stepped hurriedly back into the barn. In his haste he almost knocked down Mike Lavender. The old man had awakened to the lift of voices and had seen at least part of this.

Dick took his belt and gun from his war bag.

Lavender watched him worriedly. "You sure you know what you're doin'?"

Dick's glance touched him, then dropped away. "I don't know, Mike. I only know I've got to do *somethin'*."

Summer heat clung heavily over the empty street as Dick hurriedly walked up Center. He sensed men watching him. A remark was made just above a whisper, and he knew he was meant to overhear it. The blood rose warmly to his face, but he held his eyes straight ahead.

An idler leaning against the smoky blacksmith shop pointed a crooked finger at him. "You're runnin' the wrong way. They're in front of you, not behind you."

Choking down anger, Dick stepped up onto the long gallery of the hotel. A backward glance showed him Hornby and Collin pushing out of the saloon. Dick moved on in. The proprietor eyed him suspiciously.

"I've got to see Mrs. Matson and Nora," Dick told him.

The hotel man frowned. "Don't you think you'd better move on? I don't believe they'll care to see you."

Dick's nervous hands gripped the desk edge. "I know what you think of me. I know what the town thinks. But that doesn't matter right now. Ansel Hornby and Branch Collin are on their way here to see Mrs. Matson. She ought to know."

The man's eyes widened. "They're upstairs in seven. I'll go with you."

Dick rapped insistently on the door. Mrs. Matson pulled it inward. Her grieved eyes hardened at sight of him. "I thought you'd be gone by now. What do you want?"

He told her. Mrs. Matson's jaw was set like carved stone.

Dick finished, "I'll be here if you need me." He tried vainly to see past Mrs. Matson, perhaps for a glimpse of Nora.

Winter ice was in the tall woman's voice. "We needed you last night. We can do without you now."

Through the open door he watched her move back to a wooden dresser and reach into the drawer. Then Dick turned away. Slowly he walked down the stairs, the hotel man behind him. At the foot of the steps Dick stopped and waited. Ansel Hornby strode through the open front door and stood a moment, adjusting his eyes to the dark interior. Branch Collin came in behind him and stood at his side, mouth fixed in his usual hard grin. His eyes raked Dick in contempt.

A soft, feminine tread on the stairs behind him made Dick step aside. Mrs. Matson came down, and Nora. Dick glanced quickly at Nora. Her brown eyes sharply met his, then fell away. Her lips trembled.

In an empty gesture of politeness, Ansel Hornby removed his broad-brimmed hat and bowed slightly. Branch Collin never moved or changed expression. "Good afternoon, Mrs. Matson, Miss Matson," Hornby said. "I heard about your son. I want to tell you how deeply I regret it, ma'am."

Hatred darkened Mrs. Matson's face.

Hornby went on, "It wasn't necessary, Mrs. Matson. It isn't necessary that there be any more deaths. You could stop it."

Dick saw that her hands were trembling. One was covered by a dark brown shawl.

Hornby's voice intensified. "It's only the barbed wire, ma'am. I think I could talk to the fence cutters, if I had your assurance that the wire would not go up again. Your husband would listen. That's all it would take, just a word from you."

Mrs. Matson's voice was quiet and flat. "It's our land. It's our right to fence it. We'll be there when you're dead!"

Hornby's face began to cloud. "There'll be more killin's, Mrs. Matson. A word from you could save your men. Keep silent, and they may die."

Mrs. Matson's lips curved downward. "No, Ansel. It's *you* who will die!"

The shawl fell away. Gun metal winked a reflection from the window. For just an instant Dick froze. He saw Branch Collin's hand streak upward from his holster.

Dick leaped at Mrs. Matson, putting himself between her and Collin. He grabbed her hand and forced it down. The barrel blazed in his grip as the gun thundered and a bullet bored through the plank floor. In fury Mrs. Matson threw her body against him, struggling for the pistol. But Dick held his grip on the hot barrel and wrenched it away. It clattered to the floor at Hornby's feet. Mrs. Matson fell back against her daughter. Her face was splotched red.

"You *are* a coward. Get out of my sight. If I ever see you again, Dick Fladness, I'll kill you!"

She whirled and hurried back up the stairs. Dick flinched under the lash of contempt in Nora's dark eyes.

Collin's eyes followed the women. "Another second and I'd of shot her. Good thing for her that you did what you did, Fladness."

Dick's face twisted. "I wish I could've let her kill you, Hornby. One way or another, though, you're goin' to lose."

Hornby tried to stare him down. Branch Collin's cold grin came back, and he resembled a cat stalking a mouse. "Maybe you better apologize to Mr. Hornby."

Dick clenched his fists. "I apologize for nothin'."

Collin's hand worked down toward the pistol on his hip. "That's a good-lookin' six-shooter you're wearin', Fladness. Maybe you'd like to try to use it."

Dick went cold. "I couldn't match you, Collin."

Collin's eyes remained on him, hard as steel. "See there? You've crawfished again."

Impatiently, Hornby spoke. "What did you expect, Branch? You knew he was a coward. We'll give the boys another hour at the bar. Then we'll take a ride around the bayou and see about that wire. We're goin' to finish this thing once and for all."

He turned on his heel and strode out, his spurs ringing dully to the strike of his heavy boots. Collin faced Dick a moment more. "Another hour," he said grimly, "then we'll leave. But you better be gone before that. If you're still here, I'll leave you hangin' on the fence like any dead coyote."

A chill on his shoulders, Dick stood and listened to the fading tread of Collin's boots as the man stepped down from the gallery. Cold sweat broke on Dick's forehead and on his suddenly weak hands.

The hotel man's shaky voice broke the stillness. "That

was better than I expected of you, Fladness. But you'd best move on. You can get a far piece in an hour."

Woodenly Dick picked up Mrs. Matson's pistol from the freshly swept floor. He handed it to the hotel man. "Take it to her. She's liable to need it."

Dick stood on the hotel porch, steadying himself against a post. The heat of late afternoon rushed against him, stifling him, crushing his lungs. The street seemed stretched out of shape. It swayed back and forth, and it looked a mile long. He knew it was his nerves. They tingled like telegraph wires.

Two men stood in front of the nearby saloon. The words of one came to Dick like the slap of a swinging rope. "Bet you the drinks he lights off of that porch in a high lope."

Dick swallowed hard. Deliberately he stepped down into the street. He started back toward Lavender's barn, his steps measured and slow. He was so scared he was sick at his stomach. But they weren't going to see him run.

It seemed an hour before he gained the door of the barn. Mike Lavender's chair was empty. Dick sagged into it. Lavender hobbled up, braced his long arm against the door and leaned on it, looking out across the town and saying nothing.

"You've heard about it?" Dick asked him finally.

Mike nodded gravely. "Collin means it, Dick. I told you a while ago that you ought to stay. I've changed my mind. You better go, son. I got you a horse in the pen back yonder."

Dick stared at the ground. A thousand things hummed through his mind, memories of people he had known and ridden with and liked. He had especially liked Lindy Matson. Maybe Lindy's death was Dick's fault, and maybe it wasn't.

"You goin', or ain't you?" Mike queried anxiously.

Dick shook his head. "Give me time to study."

For a long time he sat there staring vacantly across the town. He watched a lazy cur dog make its leisurely way down the street, checking under high porches, sniffing at every corner. He watched a brown hen out back of a washerwoman's house, scratching around in the thin shade of a mesquite, seeking a cool place to settle herself.

Most of all he watched the saloon where Collin and the Hornby crew were. Occasionally he would see one or two of them come out, look around and go back in. He could feel speculative eyes appraising him from a distance, and he wondered how poor the betting odds were that he might not run.

Mike Lavender tromped back and forth in the barn like a stallion in a small corral. Now and then he would stop in the door and look up the street with Dick. Once he drew an old stem-winding watch from his pocket. "Been half an hour, Dick."

Dick nodded dully.

Mike said, "Son, I know that on a thing like this a man has got to make up his own mind. But anybody would know you ain't got much chance against a man like Branch Collin. Supposin' you leave now, there ain't much people can say that they ain't said already."

Dick never answered. He sat in the doorway, watching.

He saw the flare of a long skirt on the gallery of the hotel. The girl stood looking down the street toward the barn. Her shoulders squared as she saw Dick sitting in the doorway. Quickly she lifted the hem and rushed down the steps onto the street. In a few moments Nora Matson stood in front of him, her young face pale.

"Dick," she said huskily, "are you a fool? I thought you'd be gone by now."

Bitterness coiled in him. "Like last night?"

She flushed. "Dick, it won't help anything for you to stay here and get killed. It's too late to bring Lindy back."

He searched her eyes for some sign of the love he had seen there before. "Does it still matter to you, Nora?"

"It matters. Last night changed a lot of things, but I can't forget what there was between us. I beg you. Go!"

Dick watched her walk hurriedly back toward the hotel, drawing upon her stout pride to keep her shoulders straight and her head high. Dick looked down, staring fixedly at the ground in front of his brush-scarred boots. He heard Mike Lavender stomping around behind him.

"Mike," he said, "is that horse still out there?"

A sigh of relief passed the old cowhand's lips. "He is, and it's high time you used him."

Stiffly Dick stood up. He glanced at the saloon long enough to know he was being watched. Then he moved back into the barn and picked up his saddle and bridle. He flipped a loop over the horse's head, pulled him in, bridled and saddled him. The pen had an outside gate opening west. Going out through it, a man could leave town without using the street. But it wouldn't keep him from being seen.

Mike strode out of the barn with Dick's war bag. "Here's your gear. Good luck to you."

"Thanks, Mike," Dick replied. "But it's not me that's goin'. It's you!"

Lavender's jaw sagged. "Me? What in the—"

Dick said, "Look, Mike, you know I couldn't beat Collin if he came lookin' for me. But I'm a fair enough shot. If I had surprise on my side, I might beat him.

"You're about my size, Mike. You're goin' to spur out of this gate and head west in a lope. They'll think it's me. When Collin comes, he won't expect me. Maybe that'll be enough to give me an edge."

The old man's face was sharp with anxiety. "And maybe it won't."

Dick shrugged. "If it doesn't, I sure appreciate the way you've stuck by me."

Lavender placed his knotty hand on Dick's shoulder. "Son, I know why you ran last night. I knew all along you wasn't no coward. Good luck to you."

Dick opened the gate for him. The old man spurred out and swung westward, the dust rising beneath the horse's hoofs.

Dick watched him a minute. Then he latched the gate and hurried once again through the back door of the barn. In the shadowed interior he picked his spot, about twenty feet inside the barn door, where he would not readily be seen from outside. He pulled up a chair and sat down to wait. Holding the gun, he sat back, his hands cold with sweat, nervousness playing through him like lightning in a stormy sky. His eyes set on the open door, he waited. . . .

He heard the voices before he saw the men. They were laughing voices, lifted high by the warmth of liquor. Dick heard the easy jingling of spurs. Branch Collin and Ansel Hornby swung into view, their men trailing. Collin was laughing, and even Hornby's normally somber face showed a little humor. The sight of the horseman spurring out the back way had been a joke even Hornby could enjoy.

Still in the sunlight, Collin threw back his head and roared, "Hey, Lavender, I see we flushed your quail."

Collin and Hornby walked in through the door and passed into the shadow. Collin blinked away the momentary blindness and sought out Dick Fladness's form in the dark of the barn. Dick stood up and took one step forward from the chair.

Collin's jaw dropped as recognition hit him like the lash of a whip. His hand dipped.

But the surprise had delayed him a moment. In that moment Dick brought his pistol up into line. It exploded twice. Collin's weapon cracked once, raising a puff of dust at the man's toes just before he pitched forward onto his face.

Paralyzed, Ansel Hornby stared foolishly at Collin's sprawled form. He grabbed at his own pistol, then realized belatedly how foolish *that* was. He stopped with it half out of the holster. He stared into the smoking muzzle of Dick's six-shooter, and horror slowly crawled into his eyes as he felt death brush him.

He stammered, his voice failing as panic gripped him. "For God's sake," he managed, finally. "My God, man, don't kill me!"

Dick held his pistol steady. He had every intention of squeezing the trigger, and Hornby must have seen it in his eyes. Hornby let his pistol drop to the dust. "Fladness, for the love of God . . ." His knees gave way, and he sank to the dust, crying.

Dick looked past Hornby at Hornby's men. Muddled

with drink, they had sobered quickly at the roar of guns. They stared in disbelief upon the man who had led them, now groveling in the dust, begging for his life.

Other men gathered, and they too, stared, and they knew who was the coward.

Dusk gathered heavily. Dick sat on the broad gallery of the hotel, the cool evening breeze bringing him relief from the heat and ordeal of the day. From inside the lobby Mike Lavender's voice drifted out to him.

"You see, Mrs. Matson," Mike was saying, "it was the fire that chased Dick away last night. It was several years back that me and Dick was workin' for the same outfit. One night one of the hands got careless with a cigarette. We woke up with the bunkhouse burnin' down around us. Smoke had already knocked out a couple of the boys in their sleep.

"Wasn't time for us to do anything except run. Dick tried to drag one of the boys out, but part of the roof fell in on him. Dick was pinned under a burnin' timber that broke his leg. He laid there and seen that other boy burn to death. We finally got Dick loose just before the whole place caved in. That's where his limp come from, and his fear of fire. Most anything else he could've stood. But when the fire got to burnin' him last night, he couldn't hold out."

Presently Mrs. Matson came out onto the gallery. Nora was with her. "Dick," Mrs. Matson said, "I wish there was some way to tell you. . . ."

Hat crushed in his hands, Dick nodded. "I know."

Mrs. Matson gripped his arm. "I wish you would go hitch the team to the buckboard. I want you to take us home."

Dick shook his head. "There's not much home left out there."

Her shoulders braced. "No house, perhaps, but a house can be rebuilt. It takes more than fire to destroy a home."

Dick stepped down from the porch and started toward the livery barn.

"Wait for me," Nora said, and hurried after him. "I'd like to go with you."

Horse Well

The Jigger Y chuckwagon was camped at Horse Well the night the showdown finally came between Jeff Bowman and Cleve Sharkey. I was just a button then, not yet ten years old. The first excitement of the Crane County oil boom had simmered down in the wake of the Depression, as every Texas oil boom did sooner or later. The place had almost settled into the calm that permanency brings, as much permanency as there can ever be for a community that depends on anything as hard to put a handle on as cattle and oil.

The times were still tight, and there were some around who would turn a fast dollar whenever the opportunity arose. A Jigger Y steer butchered in the dark and peddled out by the chunk in town and in the oil camps was one way to do it.

My dad was foreman of the Y. It was his job to make the cattle operation turn a profit whether beef prices were good or not. He usually went to Midland when it came time to hire cowboys; the men in Crane were mostly working in the oil fields. Dad knew a lot of people in Midland, and there were usually some job-hunting hands waiting around the Scharbauer Hotel for a ranch owner or a foreman to show up. That was where he hired Cleve Sharkey.

The next day Cleve Sharkey came sliding his shiny green Model A coupe to a stop on the gravel in front of the L-shaped kitchen and bunkhouse. As he stepped out, I decided he was the ideal cowboy to fit all those stories the old-timers used to tell about the good old days, back when they were young. He appeared to be seven feet tall, but of course I was looking up at him from pretty low down to the ground at that time. He wore his Levi's jeans tucked into the tall tops of a fancy-stitched pair of high-heeled boots made for dancing, not for cow work. He was good-looking too, I thought, like the people in the stories I had heard old Wes Reynolds and Daddy George Lee and those others tell.

That was an early age for a boy to learn that you shouldn't judge people by what they looked like. My old pet cat Blue Boy came ambling across the bunkhouse porch, full of curiosity about the new hand, and put himself right between Cleve's feet. Cleve came near falling, and he gave Blue Boy a kick that boosted him off into the little patch of Bermuda grass at the edge of the porch.

Right there I got off to a bad start with Cleve. I told him what I thought about anybody who was mean to cats. He in turn told me what he thought about kids who mouthed off to grown-ups. My dad stepped out of our house about that time and came walking across the yard, still too far away to see that anything was wrong. Cleve carried his bedroll and war bag on into his room, and I left before Dad had a chance to challenge me about being at the bunkhouse without any business. I picked up Blue Boy and carried him out to the barn to satisfy myself that he was all right. Actually, he was too fat to hurt.

I made it a point after that to stay out of Cleve's way, though I watched him from a safe distance. He was a good cowpuncher, even if his behavior didn't fit the model I had been led to expect in a top hand. Dad had bought some rank young broncs over on the Pecos River, and Cleve rode the worst of them. He could rope a runaway cow and stand her on her rump about as well as anybody I had seen.

But he was hard on his horses. Some of the broncs lost a lot of hair where his spurs raked them.

After Cleve had been on the ranch awhile, he took to going to town pretty often. I never was much of a hand with a rope, but at the time I thought it was because I never had a chance to practice with a really good one. One Saturday evening after he had gone, I borrowed the rope from his saddle in the barn and practiced roping fenceposts. I forgot to take it in, and that night it rained.

Next afternoon Cleve found his ruined rope where I had left it hanging on a fence. It was as limber as a dishrag. But it still had plenty of sting left in it when he doubled one end and applied two or three smart licks where I would feel them the most.

One day Buddy Green quit us, and Dad had to go to Midland to hunt another cowhand. Buddy didn't say why he was leaving, but I thought I knew. For three months, when Dad wasn't around, I had seen Cleve bullying him. Buddy was a little feller who looked like he had been weaned short of his time. Cleve could have hurt him bad if he had ever taken the notion, and Buddy probably decided sooner or later he would take the notion.

I never did tell Dad about any of that. One of the first lessons he had ever taught me was to keep out of other people's business.

I was a little disappointed when Dad came back from Midland, bringing Jeff Bowman. I followed Dad's rattling old ranch pickup to the barn and watched dismally as Jeff unloaded his saddle and other tack. I had hoped Dad might bring out somebody who would whip Cleve Sharkey. At a glance I knew Jeff Bowman wasn't likely ever to do it.

He was almost as short as Buddy had been, though he was some wider in the shoulders. His clothes were nothing like Cleve's. He wore a wrinkled blue work shirt, patched khaki pants, not even Levi's, and an old hat that looked as if he had let twenty-seven horses run over it. His boot heels leaned in two directions.

He wouldn't have fit the stories I had heard from Wes and Daddy George.

Cleve rode in from the beef pasture about milking time. I happened to be making mighty quiet in the barn at the moment because Dad had been threatening to teach me to milk our Jersey cow, about as uncowboylike an activity as I could imagine. That is how I happened to be perched out of sight on top of the feed sacks when Cleve walked in carrying his saddle, his big spurs jingling. Jeff

Bowman was standing by a rack, patching a broken bridle rein. Both men stiffened as they saw each other. Cleve dropped his saddle unceremoniously to the floor.

"Jeff!" he said, after a minute. "I thought they had you in the—"

Jeff Bowman had both of his fists clenched. "I got a parole."

Cleve stammered a little. "Dammit, what did you have to come here for? You tryin' to ruin me?"

Bowman's voice cut like barbed wire. "I didn't know you were here. But anyway, you like to've ruined *me*. You didn't even have the decency to come forward and tell them the truth."

Cleve's face clouded up, as I had seen it do more than once. His fists doubled, he stepped closer to Bowman. "You ain't stayin'. You're goin' to tell the foreman you don't like the looks of this place and you want to go back to Midland."

I had always thought when people laughed, they saw something funny. Bowman laughed, and there wasn't anything funny about it. "There was a time you'd of scared me, Cleve, but not anymore. Ain't nothin' you could ever do to me worse than you've already done. I need this job. If anybody leaves, it'll be you."

Cleve bristled like a porcupine, but Bowman stared him down. Finally Cleve picked up his saddle, flung it onto a rack, and stomped out. I didn't have much idea what they were talking about. I wasn't even sure exactly what a parole was. I just knew I was going to try my best to get along with Jeff Bowman.

It turned out he was a better hand than Cleve, and he wasn't hard on his horses. More important than that, he took a lot of time trying to teach me how to use a rope. It didn't do much good, but the fault was mine, not his. I never did get the knack for it, then or later.

One day Morgan Lambert of the Cross L dropped by for a visit. He brought his daughter Ellie along. She was probably just one side or the other of twenty then. I considered her pretty old. But I considered her *pretty*, about on a par with a little girl who had sat at a desk next to mine in the third grade, one who made my face turn warm every time she spoke to me.

Jeff and Cleve felt the same way about Ellie, seemed like. Before Jeff had come, I had seen Cleve trying to butter up to her. He had no better luck with her than I had with the girl in school. But somehow it was different with Jeff. He was a long way from handsome, but she appeared to overlook that from the start. The two hit it off well as soon as my dad introduced them.

Before long Jeff was borrowing the company pickup and making trips over to the Cross L every few nights. Once in a while I would catch Cleve watching the pickup as it bounced out across the needle-grass flat to the east and disappeared around the jog in the horse-pasture fence. He looked as if he was festering up a sore.

One night a little before the Y started its fall roundup, a big dance was thrown over at the Mayfield place. Mother and Dad took us kids along. Jeff borrowed the pickup, as usual, and went after Ellie. Cleve headed for town in his Model A coupe, and after a while he brought out a town girl who wore enough rouge and lipstick to paint a barn door. She created some comment among the grown-ups, but I couldn't understand why. She reminded me of a birthday package.

It didn't take me long to get on the outs with the big Thompson boy, who was two years older and a hand-and-a-half taller than me. He was always looking for somebody to be on the outs with, and he usually won whatever contest resulted. I stayed close to the grown-ups to keep my nose clean, and listened to the fiddle music.

Cleve's girl seemed to make a lot of trips to the kitchen, and pretty soon she was wobbly on her feet. She was dancing with just about every unattached man there, though I noticed the married men didn't seem to ask her. Cleve quit asking her too.

Jeff and Ellie took most of their dances with each other. Cleve was watching them, and the devil was looking out of his eyes. Presently Jeff went to the kitchen to get Ellie some punch. Cleve pulled Ellie out onto the dance floor.

She put up a little quiet resistance, but not enough to attract much notice. There was anger in her face.

The sight made me ashamed. I pushed through the crowd and went out into the cool night air. In front of the house the big Thompson boy was daring anybody to come and wrestle with him. I had been through that with him once and didn't want any more, so I walked on out into the darkness, away from the yellow lamplight. The door opened, and Cleve came out, holding Ellie by the wrist and pulling her along.

"Now, looky here," he said, with his voice full of indignation, "I was always nice to you, but you always treated me like I was a dog with the mange. That Jeff Bowman comes along, and you take right up with him. Now I want to know, what's the matter with me?"

Cleve acted like he had been in the kitchen too many times himself.

Ellie was not one to raise her voice, but she left no doubt where she stood. "If you could see yourself right now, you'd know what's the matter. You're an egotistical—"

That was all she got to say, because Cleve pulled her to him and kissed her. She was making an angry noise and beating her little fists against him.

The door opened, and Jeff Bowman stood there against the bright lamplight. He took three or four long strides and spun Cleve around like he was a bottle-fed calf. "You take your hands off of her!" He had his fist drawn back, but Ellie grabbed his arm.

"No, Jeff, please. Let's don't have a fight and get everybody out here. It isn't worth that."

Cleve stood there looking like a whipped dog. He was sobering up in a hurry, realizing what he had done. "I'm sorry, Ellie," he said. "I've had too much to drink, or I wouldn't of touched you. I'd cut off my arm before I'd hurt you. I don't want *him* hurtin' you either, so I'm goin' to tell you. He ain't long out of jail."

Ellie looked as if he had hit her. She turned toward Jeff. "Jail?"

Cleve said, "Not just no little old county jail either. He's been in the pen at Huntsville."

Ellie stood waiting for some kind of word from Jeff, and no word came. She sounded as if she was about to cry. "Why didn't you tell me?"

"I've tried. I just couldn't. I didn't know how you'd take it."

She turned and ran back into the house, sobbing.

Cleve said, "Well, now you know how she took it."

I was awfully disappointed in Jeff, not because he had been in jail, but because he didn't hit Cleve. Jeff stayed out there a long time, rolling a cigarette, smoking it, then rolling another. Ellie's father and mother went home early, and she went with them. Pretty soon I recognized the sound of the company pickup, hitting the road back to the ranch.

Jeff and Cleve kept their distance the next day. Dad must have smelled a storm brewing up. He sent them out on separate jobs and kept them that way until time for the roundup.

It was his custom to go to Midland for extra day-help to add to the regular ranch hands and the helpful neighbors during the "works" each year. He brought back five or six, plus Tom Grammer, who had been wagon cook for the Y roundups about as long as I could remember. Dad and Tom went to work bolting the chuckbox to the wagon, and Dad sent me to fetch a monkey wrench.

I couldn't find one in any of the usual places where such tools were apt to stray. I went to the big garage and looked in the back of our car, but we didn't have one either. Cleve's green coupe was sitting there, and it occurred to me a man with a car that nice was bound to have a monkey wrench in it in case he ever had to fix a flat tire. All I found in the front was a shiny-barreled rifle he always kept there. I ran my fingers back and forth over the wonderful cold steel of it and wished I had gotten off to a better start with Cleve, so he might've let me fire it sometime.

I thought I heard Dad holler all the way from the barn. He probably hadn't, but I was always listening for him to.

That reminded me about the wrench. I got up on the back bumper and opened the trunk. It surprised me. Unlike most cars that had to travel over our dusty roads, this one was as spotless as a washerwoman's scrub board. It looked like it had been cleaned out often.

There wasn't any wrench. There was a short-handled shovel, though, and a carpenter's saw. I wondered what Cleve wanted with a saw. He never did any carpenter work.

Rolled up and shoved way back was an old section of tarpaulin. Curiosity around our place had not been restricted to the cat. I pulled the tarp out and found it had been washed lately, but it still had some dark stains. Bloodstains, they looked like, the kind on the tarp Dad always used to wrap fresh-killed beef. I was so interested in what I had found that I didn't hear Cleve come into the garage.

He grabbed me and jerked me off of the bumper, then let me fall to my knees. He bent down, and his face looked black with a flash of anger there in the half darkness. He grabbed the front of my shirt and demanded, "What do you think you're doin', prowlin' in my car?"

I tried to stammer that I was just looking for a wrench, but something was in my throat as big as an apple. My heart was pumping like the old gasoline engine that was used sometimes to pump water when the wind wasn't blowing enough to turn a windmill.

I thought Cleve was going to draw back and hit me, so I saw a little daylight off to the left side of him and ran for it as hard as my legs would carry me. I fell once and hit the ground with my face, but I was back on my feet and running while the dust still swirled. I was so scared I didn't realize I was bleeding until Jeff Bowman caught me at the corner of the bunkhouse and looked at me with a deep concern.

"Good Lord, button," he exclaimed, "what happened to you?"

I guess I looked scared, and I glanced back toward the garage in time to see Cleve come out of it. Jeff saw him too. I didn't tell him anything, but he put two and two together. He stood there and flexed his hands while his face went dark with anger.

"He hit you?" he asked.

I had to admit Cleve hadn't, but he had made me think he was going to. Jeff nodded grimly. "I wouldn't go tellin' your dad about it, if I was you. Just tell him you stumbled and fell. Cleve'll pay, when we get him where we want him."

My heart sank in disappointment. I didn't know where Jeff wanted Cleve, but I wanted him gone. A sharp suspicion began to gnaw at me. Jeff hadn't done anything about Cleve at the dance, and he wasn't doing anything about him now. Maybe Cleve had finally run his bluff on Jeff, like he had done on Buddy, not to mention *me*. I tried to shake the doubt from my mind, but it clung there like a grass burr.

As the roundup got started, camp moved from the ranch headquarters to the Mayfield place, to the Crier windmills, then over to the Magnolia trap. It was there that I heard Cleve make some remark about Ellie at the campfire. A couple of the cowboys hung their heads, embarrassed. Jeff jumped up with his fists clenched and his back stiff, but he just stood and looked at Cleve for a minute, then walked out away from the campfire, kicking soft sand with his worn-out boots.

My face burned with shame. I went off and crawled into my bedroll and pulled the tarp up over me like I expected rain. It was a long time before I went to sleep.

Finally the chuckwagon moved across the sand country and onto the chalky alkali flat toward Horse Well. That place had always fascinated me. It wasn't any different in appearance from the other camps except that it probably had the dustiest pens to brand calves in. But there *was* a difference.

About as far back as I could remember, I had heard the legend about Horse Well. One of the hands had shown me an unmarked grave over in the big south pasture. In it was buried a cowboy from way back in the 1880s, he said, killed by a band of horse thieves. The cowboy's friends had trailed the murderers, shot them all, then dumped their bodies into the deep hand-dug hole over which the windmill tower now stood at Horse Well.

Cowboys claimed that if you listened on a dark night, you could hear the dead men's spirits moan from down deep in that black hole. I had been to school and didn't really believe that kind of thing anymore. Still, that old windmill used to groan enough to make your hair stand on end, especially at night. Greasing and releathering it didn't seem to help much. Any time we camped at Horse Well I always stayed close to the wagon and kept my bedroll on the off side of it.

It was a comfort to know that Tom Grammer kept a .45 pistol in the chuckbox, though what good that would do against spirits I never had taken time to worry out.

The day the wagon moved to Horse Well, Dad sent me with Jeff on drive. Any other time that would have made me proud, because Dad usually kept me close to him so he could give me Hail Columbia when I made a mistake a-horseback, which was usually. But now I couldn't hold my eyes to Jeff without feeling that he and I shared a guilty secret.

We weren't far from camp when my horse Blackjack suddenly shied and jumped sideways. I gulped a mouthful of air and grabbed at the saddle horn too late. I got up spitting sand as Jeff caught my horse.

Smelling something putrid, I looked around to see what had boogered Blackjack. Off to the left was a hole where the wind had blown the sand away. Holding both snorting horses, Jeff swung down and took a look at it. He handed the reins to me, then poked around in the hole with a dead mesquite limb. He dragged out two sandy but fairly fresh cowhides. Beneath them were the heads and guts of two butchered cattle.

"Bet some thievin' oil fielders done it," I said indignantly, as I figured a good cowboy ought to. Anything that went wrong, it was the custom of the times to blame it on the oil fielders. Usually it turned out they had nothing to do with whatever it was.

Jeff's jaws bulged out a little, and his mouth was grim. "Yeah," he said quietly, "probably some oil fielders."

After supper, and before it got dark enough to be spooky, I borrowed Jeff's rope and went off toward the mill to practice roping fenceposts. I wanted to be far enough from the wagon that the real punchers couldn't watch me and hooraw me for missing most of my loops.

My brother Myrle came out directly. He was only about shoulder high to a Shetland pony then, and too young to know he was supposed to be scared of the place. He quickly tired of watching me miss and walked on over to peer at the old well. Pretty soon I dropped the rope and followed him, leaving the loop still attached to a fencepost, which I had caught from a distance of at least five or six feet. I thrilled as I looked at the wooden tower, and let my imagination carry me back to the good old days of high adventure.

Myrle spoiled it. He leaned over the wide hole and said eagerly, "Bet you if we had us a lantern we could look down there and see the skeletons."

The hair on the back of my neck began to bristle, and I suddenly noticed dusk was gathering around us. I said, "Tom probably wants us to help him dry up the utensils."

Not until we were back at the wagon did I remember that I had left Jeff's rope hanging from a fencepost. I had no intention of going back for it, because dark was closing in.

Car lights began showing through the gloom. A man from Crane came bouncing up in a Model T. I had seen him at some ball games, selling people something to drink out of a fruit jar, and I remembered once seeing him and Cleve talking together on the sidewalk in town. He called Cleve off to one side. I could hear them arguing, though the words were not clear, and Cleve was waving his arms a lot. In a little while Cleve came up to the campfire and said to Dad, "I got some business in town that won't wait. Be all right if I go with Albert here?"

Dad nodded, and Cleve rode off in the bootlegger's old car. A look passed across Jeff's face, one I had seen a few times in camp when some cowboy won a big poker hand and raked in all the matches.

I didn't sleep very well that night. The mill got to groaning louder and louder, and I could almost hear those old horse thieves crying for help. The night closed in on me, thick as pudding and dark as a sack of black cats. I could hear voices, fighting voices. I awoke and sat straight up, throwing back the tarp. It had all been a dream.

Or maybe it hadn't. The voices were still there, muffled and distant, but I could hear them though I had both eyes wide open. I recognized Jeff's voice. For just a second a fanciful notion struck me that the spirits had come up out of that well and somehow gotten ahold of him. The notion passed as I came completely awake.

Somebody was fighting with Jeff, though; I could tell that by the sounds. My pulse racing, I pulled on my boots to keep from stepping barefooted into a patch of goatheads, then moved cautiously toward the voices, my throat as dry as old leather. I had slept in my shirt, but a cool night breeze brought goose pimples to my bare legs.

It was not so dark as I had thought. A full moon was up. In a minute I could tell the other voices didn't belong to any spirits. They were Cleve's, and the bootlegger Albert's. Jeff held Tom Grammer's big .45 in his hand and had the two men backed up against the Model T.

"I was ready to forget about goin' to jail for what you did, Cleve," he said bitterly, "but you changed my mind for me the night of the dance. I've taken a lot from you since then because I was waitin' for you to make a real mistake. It's plain to me what you've been doin' with the stuff the kid found in your car. These nights folks thought you was in town, you've been out spotlightin' and shootin' Y cattle for your friend here to peddle."

I was so relieved that I almost forgot and showed myself. It had hurt, thinking Jeff was letting Cleve put a bluff across on him.

Jeff said, "You haven't had time tonight to clean up that Model T. I expect a cattle inspector is goin' to be awful interested in what he finds there. And you can't move it without this key." He held the key up for Cleve to see, then pitched it off into the brush.

Cleve had quit talking, and I thought Albert was going to sink into a dead faint. "Now looky here, cowboy," he begged, his voice quavering, "don't you wake up the foreman. I'll pay you every cent I got in my pocket—close to a hundred dollars."

Jeff shook his head. "The only pay I want is to see Cleve go to jail, like he let me do."

Somehow it didn't seem to me that Cleve looked as worried as he ought to. He looked past Jeff and said, "All right, boys, I reckon you've heard it all."

Jeff was a cowboy, not a lawman, or he probably wouldn't have fallen for that stunt. He looked back, thinking some of the hands had come up behind him. Cleve bowled him over with his fist. The pistol fell to the ground.

Jeff and Cleve waded into each other, fighting like a couple of strapping big bulls. To be as much smaller as he was, Jeff was putting up a mighty good scrap. The brush popped and cracked as they struggled back and forth through it.

The gun still lay on the ground, its barrel gleaming in the moonlight. My heart pounded as I looked at the thing, deadly as a rattlesnake. I reached for it twice, then drew back my shaking hands. Finally I made myself pick it up.

The bootlegger was on his hands and knees, frantically searching for the key Jeff had thrown away.

I didn't know much about pistols, and I never had touched Tom's .45 before. In my nervousness I must have touched the trigger, because it exploded in my hands with a great roar and the biggest flash of fire I had ever seen. The recoil sent it flying off into the dry weeds. Not for a hundred dollars in silver would I have picked it up again.

A commotion started down at the wagon as the shot woke everybody up.

Jeff and Cleve were still fighting. Cleve had picked up a piece of a discarded windmill sucker rod and was swinging the heavy metal end of it. A good lick with that thing could brain a mule. Jeff was backing away, trying to keep beyond reach. He stumbled over something—his rope that I had left hanging from a post. For a second it looked as if Cleve had him, but Jeff jumped to his feet, one end of that rope in his hand, and made a run around Cleve. Cleve got the sucker rod caught in that rope and dropped it.

They were fighting again then, slugging it out, moving closer and closer to the old well. Boards had been nailed around the base of the tower to keep cattle from falling into the hole, but the boards were rotten. Jeff took some hard licks from Cleve but finally ducked, leaned down, and came up with a hard fist from about the level of his boot tops. It slammed Cleve back against those old boards, and he broke through. With a wild yell he tumbled backward into that deep, dark hole.

His body hit the big pipe casing as he slid down, and somehow he managed to get his arms around it. I could hear his shirt ripping as he hugged the casing and tried to stop his fall.

In a moment his voice floated upward, broken with panic. "Throw me a rope! Hurry up, or I'll lose my hold."

Several cowboys got on Jeff's rope and helped haul Cleve up out of the well. He was dirty and torn, trembling and sniffling. It was a poor time to think of such things, but I desperately wanted to ask him if he had seen anything of those old horse thieves while he was down there. I had the good judgment not to bring the matter up.

Cleve was too shaken to talk, but his friend Albert wasn't. He told it about the way Jeff had guessed.

The Y lost two hands then, Cleve to the sheriff, Jeff to the man he had worked for before he had been sent away for the cattle stealing Cleve had done. The rancher came down to the Y and apologized for past misunderstandings. He offered Jeff a foreman's job at top pay—what passed for top pay in those days anyway.

We kept seeing Jeff regularly for a while after that because he had to come through the Y to get over to the

Lambert place and visit Ellie. After they were married he didn't have that excuse anymore.

We never did see Cleve after that, so I never had the chance—if I had ever gotten the nerve—to ask him about the horse thieves in that old well.

Duster

Hamp Bowdre listened to the auctioneer's machine-gun voice as a dozen drouth-stricken sheep clattered out onto the scales. A chilly west wind whistled through the cracks in the plank siding of the auction barn. His corded right hand squeezed his left shoulder. Damned rheumatism—sign of another norther coming. It'd be a dry one—like the rest of them had been.

One of the ring men grabbed a ewe and peeled her lips back.

"Now, boys," the man said enthusiastically, "most of these ewes has got good mouths. They been on hard West Texas country, but they're bred for March lambs and worth ten dollars if they're worth a dime."

"Five dollars!" the bid starter shouted. The auctioneer picked it up from there. He wheedled and bluffed and let a sour-faced San Angelo trader have them for five-and-a-half.

Hamp took a tally book from his pocket and jotted a note. He was conscious of a knotty old cowpuncher beside him.

"Howdy, Hamp. They've sure lowered the boom on the livestock market."

Hamp frowned at the intrusion.

Eby Gallemore prodded, "What you keepin' books for?" Hamp drew up within himself. Eby could ask more questions than a prying old woman.

"You ain't figgerin' on buyin' some sheep for yourself, are you, Hamp?" Eby laughed as if he had just told a big joke. "You'll never own a sheep or a cow-brute as long as you live. You're just a wore-out old ranch hand who'll work for wages till they nail you up in a box. Like me."

Sudden impatience lashed at Hamp. "If I was like you, Eby, I'd poke a rag in my mouth and keep it there!" He stood up stiffly and hobbled out.

Eyes narrowed against the bite of dust, he watched wind whip sand off the road and whisk it away. He clenched his fist. Dammit, if it would only rain!

Eby Gallemore's words were still running through his mind. *Wore out. Never own a sheep or a cow-brute as long as you live.* Hamp's jaw ridged under his wrinkled brown skin. They'd soon see if Hamp Bowdre was wore out.

The boss came for him by and by. Crawling into the rattly old pickup truck, Hamp could see bad news carved deep into Charlie Moore's young face.

"It's all over with, Hamp," the boss finally spoke. "They're closin' me out."

Hamp couldn't say he was surprised. After four years of bare ranges, ruinous feed bills, and plummeting livestock prices, the wonder was that the bank had stayed with Charlie this long.

"I told old Prewett my lease contract is up at the end of this month—that I'd be needin' feed money besides. But he couldn't go, Hamp. Bank examiner's been crawlin' all over him about these big livestock loans he's stuck with. Well, I flipped my lid—told him if that's the way it stood, they're his sheep, and his cattle."

Moore's chin was low, his gray eyes sick. "Prewett's been good to me, and I oughtn't to've done it, Hamp. But I did. So it's the bank's outfit now—soon as they get out and take count."

Hamp didn't say anything. He didn't know anything that would help.

Moore said, "I'd rather pull my own teeth than tell Vera. She really loves that ranch—her and the kids."

Hamp nodded sympathetically. The ranchman was in his mid-thirties, fully twenty years younger than Hamp. The year Moore had come home from the war he'd borrowed money to buy livestock and lease this ranch from old Whisky Sam O'Barr. The next year, he'd hired Hamp.

"Gonna hate to part with you, Hamp," Charlie said disconsolately. "We've been a great team."

Yes, Hamp thought, they sure had. Well, it wasn't the first time drouth had done him out of a job.

As they drove over the cattle guard onto Moore's mesquite-dotted pasture, Hamp thumbed at a windmill whose tower barely showed through the haze of dust. "We better take a look at that Lodd mill. It's been weakenin'."

Out of habit, Hamp first boogered two sheep away from a feed bunk and peeped under the lid to see how much cottonseed meal and salt mixture was in it. Enough for three or four days, he noted. Sheep couldn't last long on bare range without supplemental feed. The salt was to keep them from taking too much at one time. But it took lots of water, or a sheep would dehydrate on meal and salt.

They found the mill pumping a weak stream about the size of a pencil. "Drouth's droppin' the water table," Hamp observed. "The well needs to be deepened fifteen, twenty feet."

Moore shrugged. "That's Sam O'Barr's worry now—and the bank's."

Hamp cast a worried glance at Charlie. He'd never heard that grudging tone from the boss before. He walked over and looked in the concrete storage tank. Half empty. Sheep were drinking up the water faster than it was coming out of the ground.

A cloud of dust boiled toward them on the two-rut road. An oil-field pump truck with a big water tank on back pulled up beside the windmill. A college-age kid in oil-stained work clothes stepped out from behind the wheel and eyed the two ranchmen warily. "Truck's heatin'. Needs some water in the radiator."

Suspicion began working in Hamp. That concrete tank ought not to've been so low on water. Casually he edged over to the truck and put his hand on the front of it. Warm, but not hot. Anyway, a big twenty-gallon can of drinking water was strapped on the side.

"You're from that drillin' outfit over across the fence, ain't you?" he queried. The youngster nodded.

"You-all have got a contract to take what water you need from Old Man Longley's wells. But it's a far piece over to Longley's, and it's just a mile over here. Ain't that right?"

The youngster looked as if he'd been caught sport roping another man's calves.

Hamp shook a stubby finger at him. "Now you hop in that truck and git! You ain't gonna steal another load of water here just because you're too triflin' lazy to go git it where you're supposed to."

Hamp watched until the truck was gone. "Two more truckloads would drain that tank. And we'd have a bunch of salt-poisoned sheep."

"The bank's sheep," Moore said.

Hamp eyed him sharply. Charlie acted as if he wouldn't care.

At the ranch Charlie drove the pickup into the shed. "Would you feed the stock for me, Hamp? I've got to talk to Vera."

Hamp forked some hegari bundles across the fence to a half-dozen saddle horses and a couple of potbellied dogie calves. Charlie's cowboy sons, Mackey and Jim, had finished milking the Jersey cow and were feeding their lambs. Hamp leaned against the fence and watched them with a glow of satisfaction. It was almost as if they were his own boys.

"Hey, Hamp, looky here at old Hungry," called ten-year-old Jim, proudly petting a thick-bodied Rambouillet lamb. "County agent was out today. He said you did a good job of doctorin'. Old Hungry's gonna win that San Angelo show."

Hamp nodded, but he didn't grin with Jim. Chances were they wouldn't be making the San Angelo show now. He hobbled off to the frame bunkshack that served him as a home. It was bare except for an old dresser and a cot, and a table in the corner. But it was all Hamp needed— all he wanted. He pulled the light cord and sat down at the table.

He tore a sheet off of a writing tablet and began scrawling figures. One thousand sheep at five-and-a-half—five thousand five hundred dollars. Fifteen sections of land at forty-five cents per acre lease—four thousand three hundred twenty.

He had done it so many times lately that he had all the figures in his head. But it brought him satisfaction to mark them down on paper.

Old. Wore out. Never own a sheep or a cow-brute as long as you live.

He grinned without knowing it. They wouldn't say that again.

He wondered how Eby Gallemore's eyes would pop if Hamp showed him a savings account book adding up to more than twenty-three thousand dollars.

Hamp Bowdre still had sixty cents out of every dollar he'd ever made. While Gallemore and his kind had drunk up their wages, or spent them on women, or pooped them off around the rodeos, Hamp Bowdre had been living like a monk, saving against a time when he could be his own boss.

He'd had many chances these last few years, but Hamp was a cautious man. He'd seen this boom-and-bust business before. Wait till the bust. Wait till everybody else wants to sell.

Well, they wanted to sell now. Four years of drouth and demoralized markets had done that.

It was going to rain this spring. Hamp had been through drouths before, and somehow he knew. It would rain, and the livestock business would start a slow but steady upward climb.

Maybe he could get *this* place, he was thinking. Now that Charlie Moore was dropping out, it was possible. Talk around town was that hard-drinking Sam O'Barr had spent all his money and was getting desperate. Since that wildcat oil bunch had drilled two dry holes on his ranch, the oil-lease money had petered out. Only the land lease was left. Charlie had been paying sixty cents an acre—too high the way things had turned out.

I'll offer Sam forty-five cents, Hamp thought. *He'll snuff and stomp, but bare and dry as the place is, he won't find anybody else to take it. Maybe someday I'll even find me a rich partner. . . .*

The two boys came to the shack to call Hamp for supper. A tear rolled down Jim's freckled cheek. Mackey, a year older, was gravely quiet.

"Hamp," Jim burst out, "what am I gonna do with old Hungry? Daddy says we're fixin' to move to town."

Hamp patted the boy on the head. Sure tough on the kids.

Tough on Vera too. With dancing blue eyes, and a little on the plump side, she was usually quick to laugh, but there was no fun in her tonight.

Hamp ate the cobbler pie she had baked especially for him, but he couldn't enjoy it. Vera had always been as concerned about him as if he belonged to her family. She had often made him regret he'd never married.

Hamp thought he'd probably hire him a Mexican couple if he got this place. But he was going to miss the Moores.

The next morning Charlie Moore was sick. Moody and sleepless, he had taken a long walk in the night air. Now he was fighting off the flu.

Banker Prewett was out shortly after noon the second day and found him sitting up in the living room. "Mind if I look the sheep over?" he asked.

"Have at it," Charlie answered, a little curtly. "They're your sheep."

Hamp frowned. He'd never seen Charlie act this way before, and he didn't like it. He'd thought better of Charlie.

The wind buffeted the pickup around as Hamp slowly drove the banker over the bare, dusty pastures. Prewett was studiously silent during most of the ride. "I hate to do this," he said finally. "Charlie Moore's a good man, Hamp. I'd like to've helped him."

Hamp nodded. He'd thought about lending Charlie enough money to pull him through. But it would take Charlie years to pay it back, and Hamp was getting too old to wait. If he was to get a place for himself, it had to be soon.

Hamp said suddenly, "Mr. Prewett, would the bank take five-and-a-half a head for these sheep—the whole outfit?"

Surprised, Prewett straightened. "It might. Who's interested?"

"I am." Briefly Hamp explained his idea. Prewett nodded in silent admiration. Hamp had it figured out to a T.

Their last stop was the Lodd mill. Hamp knew something was wrong—the sheep were all gathered around it.

"She's gone dry," he exclaimed.

The mill had stopped pumping. Sheep nuzzled vainly at the dried mud in the trough. The concrete tank was drained.

Hamp's face flushed red as he saw where the truck had backed up to the tank. Water had sloshed out over the side, and the heavy tires had left deep prints in the dried mud.

Anger clenched Hamp's knotty fists as he walked out through the bleating sheep, the blowing sand gritty in his eyes, nose, and ears. He knew it would take days to get anything out of the drilling company.

But these ewes were already drawing up. They had been without water a day or two—and with all that salt in them. They had to be taken somewhere today or they'd begin losing some unborn lambs.

Hamp made good time in getting back to the house. The banker stood by while Hamp told Charlie what had happened.

Pale, sitting weakly in his chair, Charlie frowned, looking out the north window. "It'd be hard to drive them in this norther, mighty hard. It'd be blowin' up a storm by the time anybody could get to that well a-horseback."

The banker spoke up, "Like you said, Charlie, they're the bank's sheep. I wouldn't ask you to ride out in the face of that storm. We'll just write off those lambs."

Charlie kept frowning. Suddenly he stood up and headed for the coat rack. "Catch up the horses, Hamp," he said. "The quicker we start, the quicker we get those sheep to water."

Vera grabbed Charlie's arm. "Charlie, you're sick. You can't. . . ."

But Charlie was pulling on his coat. Watching him, Hamp felt a glow begin inside him. He forgot he'd ever been disappointed in Charlie Moore.

The huge brown dust cloud was rapidly swelling out of the north. For the three horsemen, riding into it was like heading into the mouth of a gigantic howling cave. Prewett rode with Charlie and Hamp—he had been a ranch hand before he had been a banker. It took an hour or more to reach the mill. By that time Hamp's sand-burned eyes were afire with pain.

Throwing the sheep into a bunch was a hard job. It's the nature of sheep to drift into the wind, unless it's too strong. Heading the ewes away from it at an angle took the hardest chousing Hamp had ever done in his life. The only way to turn them was to ride along beside them, whipping at their faces with an empty gunnysack.

The wind lifted to a new fury, the dust so thick that sometimes Hamp couldn't see Charlie fifteen feet away. It became too much for the sheep. They wanted to stop and huddle in helpless confusion.

Desperation swelled and grew in Hamp. He dismounted, and leading his horse, went to shoving against them, slapping at them with his bare hands. Hope flagging, he pulled over beside Charlie and shouted, "It's no use. Let's let them go."

Charlie was walking too, bent painfully, stumbling over his own feet. But doggedly he shook his head. "No! We'll fight them a little longer."

Hamp pulled back and went to shoving again, shouting until the voice finally left him. But somehow they were getting the job done. They had the sheep angled toward the house. And they were keeping them moving.

They finally struck a net-wire fence, and it was easier after that. Through one gate, then another, dragging one ewe so the others would follow.

It was dark when they shoved the last ewe through the gate at the headquarters, and the sheep bunched up around the two long water troughs in the holding corral. Hamp saw that Charlie was smiling. Then Charlie's legs buckled.

In the house, Vera had a pot of coffee on the stove, hot and waiting. Wearily Hamp and Prewett sat with steaming cups in their hands, watching Vera go back and forth to and from the room where they had put Charlie. The kids sat quietly with their lessons, but they weren't studying much. Hamp coughed from deep in his throat. Vera hovered over him worriedly, telling him she'd better put some medicine down him or he would be sick like Charlie.

"I'll be okay," Hamp told her hoarsely, his throat raw. "I'm just give out, and got a chestful of dust. It's the same with Charlie. He'll cough it out."

She forced a smile. "Maybe, Hamp, maybe. The point is, he just doesn't care now. Losing this ranch and all . . ."

The idea had come to Hamp somewhere in that long drive, and it had grown with every step he had taken back toward the house. He'd need a good partner—and right here he could get a partner who had something better than money. Charlie had been sick. He hadn't had to go out there in the face of a duster, to save sheep that didn't belong to him anymore. But he had gone.

"Looky here, Vera," Hamp said, "you-all don't have to lose this place. You could take on a partner."

Her blue eyes widened. "A partner?"

"Me." He explained to her about the money he had saved, about the plan he'd had to take over the ranch when they left. "With the money I've got, we can pay Mr. Prewett here enough to satisfy the examiner. We can feed these sheep till it rains in the spring. And leave it to me to whittle Sam O'Barr down on the lease; I can be mean when I have to.

"It'll take the range a long time to recover, but the sheep that're still on the place now can be a foundation for us to start with. We can let the flock grow back as the range does."

Excitement bubbled within him. "What do you think, Vera? Reckon Charlie would take me on as a partner, fifty-fifty?"

The two kids were grinning. Vera's round face was all

mixed up, her eyes laughing and crying at the same time. "He will, Hamp," she said. "I know he will."

Hamp walked out onto the front porch where the wall sheltered him from the wind. Prewett followed him. Hamp rolled a brown-paper cigarette while the banker stuffed his pipe. The wind howled as if there was nothing between there and the North Pole but a barbed-wire fence.

Well, let it blow. Pretty soon it would be spring, and things would change.

In the darkness he could sense the banker smiling at him.

Defensively Hamp said, "I always *have* wanted a place of my own. And I used to wish I had me a family. Well, sir, I've got that too. What better could a wore-out old ranch hand ask, for just twenty-three thousand dollars?"

The Debt of Hardy Buckelew

I guess you'd call him crazy. We did, that spring of '78 when old man Hardy Buckelew set out to square his account against the Red River.

That was my third year to help graze the Box H steer herd from South Texas up the Western Trail toward Dodge. The first year I had just been the wrangler, bringing up the remuda to keep the riders in fresh mounts. A button job, was all. The second year they promoted me. Didn't matter that they put me back at the dusty tail end of the herd to push up the drags. It was a cowboy job, and I was drawing a man's wages, pretty near.

Old Hardy Buckelew had only one son—a big, raw-boned, overgrown kid by the name of Jim, wilder than a Spanish pony. They used to say there was nothing Jim Buckelew couldn't whip, and if anything ever did show up, old man Hardy would whip it for him. That's the way the Buckelews were.

I never did see but one thing Jim couldn't whip.

He was only nineteen the first time I saw him. That young, he wasn't supposed to be going into saloons and suchlike. He did anyway; he was so big for his age that nobody paid him much mind. Or if they did notice him, maybe they knew they'd have to throw him out to get rid of him. That wouldn't have been much fun.

One time in San Antonio he fell into a card game with a pair of sharpers, and naturally they fleeced him. He raised

112

a ruckus, so the two of them throwed together and lit into him. They never would have whipped him if the bartender in cahoots with them hadn't busted a bottle over Jim's head.

Now, a man who ever saw old Hardy Buckelew get mad would never forget it as long as he lived. He was one of those old-time Texas cowmen—the likes of which the later generations never saw. He stood six feet tall in his brush-scarred boots. He had a hide as tough as the mesquite land he rode in and a heart as stout as a black Mexican bull. When he hollered at a man, his voice would carry a way yonder, and you could bet the last dollar you owned that whoever he hollered at would come a-running too.

Old Hardy got plenty mad that time, when Jim came limping in broke and bruised and bloody. The old man took him way off to one side for a private lecture, but we could hear Hardy Buckelew's bull voice as far as we could see him.

Next day he gathered up every man he could spare, me included, and we all rode a-horseback to San Antonio. We marched into the saloon where the fight had taken place and marched everybody else out—everybody but the bartender and the two gamblers. They were talking big, but their faces were white as clabber. Old Hardy busted a bottle over the bartender's head and laid him out colder than a wedge. Then he switched those fiery eyes of his to Jim Buckelew and jabbed his stubby thumb in the direction of the gamblers.

"Now this time," he said, "do the job right!"

Jim did. When we left there, three men lay sprawled in the wet sawdust. Jim Buckelew was grinning at us, showing a chipped front tooth like it was a medal from Jeff Davis himself. His knuckles were torn and red-smeared as he counted out the money he had taken back from the gamblers' pockets.

Old man Hardy's voice was rough, but you couldn't miss the edging of pride in it. "From now on, Jimbo, whether it's a man or a job, don't you ever take a whippin' and quit. No matter how many times it takes, a Buckelew keeps on comin' back till he's won."

Now then, to the debt of Hardy Buckelew.

Late in the summer of '77 we finished a cow hunt and
threw together a herd of Box H steers to take to Kansas
and the railroad before winter set in. Hardy Buckelew never
made the trip himself anymore—too many years had stacked
up on him. For a long time now, Will Peril had been his
trail boss. Will was a man a cowboy liked to follow—a
graying, medium-sized man with the years just commencing
to put a slump in his shoulders. His voice was as soft as the
hide of a baby calf, and he had a gentle way with horses
and cattle. Where most of us might tear up enough ground
to plant a potato patch, Will Peril could make livestock do
what he wanted them to without ever raising the dust.

He handled men the same way.

This time, though, Hardy Buckelew slipped a joker in
the deck.

"Will," Hardy said, "it's time Jimbo took on a man's
responsibilities. He's twenty-one now, so I'm puttin' him
in charge of this trail herd. I just want you to go along and
kind of keep an eye on him. You know, give him his head
but have one hand on the reins, just in case."

Will Peril frowned, twisting his mule-hide gloves and
looking off to where the cook was loading the chuckwagon.
"Some men take longer growin' up than others do, Hardy.
You really think he's ready?"

"You want to teach a boy to swim, you throw him in
where the water's deep. Sure he'll make some mistakes,
but the education he gets'll be worth the price."

So we pointed them north with a new trail boss in
charge. Now, Jim was a good cowboy, make no mistake
about that; he was just a shade wild, is all. He pushed too
fast and didn't give the cattle time enough to graze along
and put on weight as they walked. He was reckless too, in
the way he rode, in the way he tried to curb the stampedes
we had before we got the cattle trailbroke. He swung in
front of the bunch one night, spurring for all he was worth.
His horse stepped in a hole and snapped its leg with a sound
like a pistol shot. For a minute there, we thought Jim was
a goner. But more often than not a running herd will split

around a man on foot. They did this time. Jim just walked away laughing. He'd have spit in the devil's eye.

All in all, Jim did a better job than most of us hands thought he would. That is, till we got to the Red River.

It had been raining off and on for three days when we bunched the cattle on the south bank of the Red. The river was rolling strong, all foamy and so muddy you could almost walk on it. You could hear the roar a long time before you got there.

The trail had been used a lot that year, and the grass was grazed down short. Will Peril set out downriver to find feed enough that we could hold the cattle while we waited for the water to run down. He was barely out of sight when Jim Buckelew raised his hat and signaled for the point man to take cattle out into the river.

"You're crazy, Jim!" exclaimed the cook, a limping old Confederate veteran by the name of Few Lively. "A duck couldn't stay afloat in that water!"

But Jim might have had cotton in his ears for all the attention he paid. When the point man held back, Jim spurred his horse out into that roaring river with the same wild grin he had when he waded into those San Antonio gamblers. Him shaming us that way, there was nothing the rest of us could do but follow in behind him, pushing the cattle.

The steers didn't like that river. It was all we could do to force them into it. They bobbed up and down, their heads out of the water and their horns swaying back and forth like a thousand old-fashioned rocking chairs. The force of the current started pulling them downriver. Up at the point, Jim Buckelew was fighting along, keeping the leaders swimming, pushing them for the far bank.

For a while there it looked like we might make it. Then, better than halfway across, the lead steers began to tire out. They still had heart in them, but tired legs couldn't keep fighting that torrent. Jim Buckelew had a coiled rope in his hand, slapping at the steers' heads, his angry voice lost in the roar of the flood. It was no use; the river had them.

And somehow Jim Buckelew lost his seat. We saw him splash into the muddy water, so far out yonder that no one could reach him. We saw his arms waving, saw him go under. Then we lost sight of him out there in all that foam, among those drowning cattle.

The heart went out of all of us. The main part of the herd milled and swam back. It was all we could do to get ourselves and the cattle to the south bank. Not an animal made it to the far side.

It was all over by the time Will Peril returned. We spent the next day gathering cattle that had managed to climb out way yonder down the river. Along toward evening, as the Red dropped, we found Jim Buckelew's body where it had washed in with an uprooted tree. We wrapped him in his blankets and slicker and dug a grave for him. A gentle rain started again like a quiet benediction as Will Peril finished reading over him out of the chuckbox Bible.

The burial done, we stood there numb with shock and grief and chill. Will Peril stuck the Bible inside his shirt, beneath the slicker.

"We haven't got a man to spare," he said tightly, "but somebody's got to go back and tell Hardy."

His eyes fell on me.

It had been bad enough, watching Jim Buckelew die helpless in that boiling river. In a way it was even worse, I think, standing there on the gallery of the big house with my hat all wadded up in my hand, watching old Hardy Buckelew die inside.

He never swayed, never showed a sign of a tear in his gray eyes. But he seemed somehow to shrink up from his six feet. That square, leather face of his just seemed to come to pieces. His huge hands balled into fists, then loosened and began to tremble. He turned away from me, letting his gaze drift out across the sun-cured grass and the far-stretching tangle of thorny mesquite range that he had planned to pass down to Jim. When he turned back to me, he was an old man. An old, old man.

"The cattle," he whispered, "did Jim get them across?"

I shook my head. "No, sir, we lost a couple hundred head. The rest got back to the south bank."

"He never did quit, though, did he? Kept on tryin' all the way?"

"He never quit till he went under, Mister Buckelew."

That meant a lot to him, I could tell. He asked, "Think you could find Jimbo's grave for me?"

"Yes, sir, we marked it."

The old man's voice seemed a hundred miles away, and his mind too. "Get some rest, then. We'll leave at daylight."

Using the buckboard, we followed the wide, tromped-out cattle trail all the way up to the Red River. We covered more ground in one day than the herd had moved in three or four. And one afternoon we stood beside Jim Buckelew's grave. The cowboys had put up a little brush fence around it to keep trail cattle from walking over it and knocking down the marker.

The old man stood there a long time with his hat in his hand as he looked at his son's resting place. Occasionally his eyes would lift to the river, three hundred yards away. The water had gone down now. The Red moved along sluggish and sleepy, innocent as could be. The dirty high-water marks of silt and debris far up on the banks were all that showed for the violence we had seen there.

Then it was that I heard Hardy Buckelew speak in a voice that sent fingers of ice crawling up my spine. He wasn't talking to me.

"I'll be back, Jimbo. Nothin' has ever beat a Buckelew. We got a debt here, and it's goin' to be paid. You watch, Jimbo, I'll be back!"

I had never really been afraid of Hardy Buckelew before. But now I saw something in his face that made me afraid, a little bit.

He turned toward the buckboard. "Let's go home," he said.

All those days of traveling for that single hour beside the river. And now we were going home again.

* * *

The old man wasn't the same after that. He stayed to himself, getting grayer and thinner. When he rode out, he went alone and not with the boys. He spent a lot of his time just puttering around the big house or out at the barn, feeding and currying and petting a roan colt that had been Jim's favorite. He never came to the cookshack anymore. The ranch cook sent his meals up to the big house, and most of the food would come back uneaten.

When the trail crew finally returned from Dodge City, old Hardy didn't even come out. Will Peril had to take his report and the bank draft up to the big house.

Will was shaking his head when he came to the cookshack for supper. Worry was in his eyes. "The thing's eatin' on him," he said, "turnin' him in on himself. I tell you, boys, if he don't get off of it, it'll drive him out of his mind."

Knowing how much Will loved that old cowman, I didn't feel like telling him what Hardy had said at the grave by the Red River. The way I saw it, Hardy Buckelew was pretty far gone already.

When winter came on, he just seemed to hole up in the big house. He didn't come out much, and when he did we wished we hadn't seen him. For a time there, we didn't expect him to live through the winter. But spring came and he was still with us. He began coming down to the cookshack sometimes, a living ghost who sat at the end of the long table, deaf and blind to what went on around him.

Time came for the spring cow hunt. Hardy delegated all of his responsibility to Will Peril, and the chuckwagon moved out.

"He won't live to see this roundup finished," Will said. You could see the tears start in his eyes. "One of these days we'll have to quit work to come in and bury him."

But Will was wrong. As the new grass rose, so did Hardy Buckelew. The life that stirred the prairies and brought green leaves to the mesquite brush seemed to touch the old man too. You could see the change in him from one day to the next, almost. He strengthened up, the flesh coming back to his broad shoulders and his square face. He commenced visiting the wagon more and more often, until one day he brought out his bedroll and pitched it on the ground along with ours.

We thought then that we had him back—the same old Hardy Buckelew. But he wasn't the same. No, sir, he was another man.

The deep lines of grief that had etched into his face were still there, and we knew they would never fade. Some new fire smouldered in his eyes like camp coals banked for the night. There was hatred in that fire, yet we saw nothing for him to hate. What had happened was nobody's fault.

As the strength came back to him, he worked harder than any man in the outfit. Seemed like he never slept. More often than not, he was the one who woke up the cook of a morning and got the coffeepot on to boil. He was always on the go, wearing out horses almost as fast as we could bring them up for him.

"Tryin' to forget by drivin' himself into the grave," Will Peril said darkly. "I almost wish he was still mopin' around that ranch house."

So did some of the others. Hardy got so hard to follow that three of his cowboys quit. Two reps for other outfits left the Box H wagon and swore they wouldn't come back for anything less than his funeral. Hardy didn't even seem like he noticed.

We finished the regular spring works, and we had a sizable bunch of big steers thrown together for the trip up the trail to Dodge. For those of us who usually made the drive, it was a welcome time. We were tickled to death at the idea of getting away from Hardy Buckelew awhile. I think even Will Peril, much as he thought of the boss, was looking forward to a little breathing spell himself.

We spent several days getting the outfit ready. We put a fresh trail brand on the steers so that if they ever got mixed up with another bunch we could know them easy. We wouldn't have to stretch a bunch of them out with ropes and clip away the hair to find the brands.

You could tell the difference in the men as we got ready. There wasn't much cheer among those fixing to stay home, but the trail crew was walking around light as feathers. Trail driving being the hard, hot, dusty, sleepless, and once-in-a-while dangerous work that it is, I don't know why anybody would look forward to it. But we did.

The night before we started, Hardy Buckelew dropped us the bad news. He was going too.

Will Peril argued with him till he was blue in the face. "You know what it's like to go up that trail, Hardy—you've done it often enough. You're not in any condition to be makin' the trip."

Will Peril was the only man Hardy Buckelew ever let argue with him, and even Will didn't do it much.

"Who owns this outfit?" Hardy asked.

"You do," Will said.

"What part of this outfit is yours?"

"None of it," Will admitted.

"Then shut up about it. I'm goin', and if you don't like it you can stay home!"

Right about then I imagine Will was tempted to. But you could see the trouble in his eyes as he studied Hardy Buckelew. He couldn't let the old man get off on that trail without being around someplace to watch out for him.

Hardy didn't bother anybody much the first few days. It was customary to drive the cattle hard the first week or so. Partly that was to get them off the range they were used to and reduce the temptation for them to stray back. Partly it was to keep them too tired to run at night till they were used to trail routine.

Hardy rode up at swing position, leaving everybody pretty much alone. Once in a while you would see him turn in the saddle and look back, but he didn't have anything to say. Seemed like everything suited him—at first.

But one morning after we had been on the trail a week he changed complexion. As we strung the cattle off the bedgrounds, Will Peril told the point man to slow them down. "We got them pretty well trailbroke," he said. "We'll let them start puttin' on a little weight now."

But Hardy Buckelew came riding up like a Mexican bull looking for a fight. "You don't do no such of a thing! We'll keep on pushin' them!"

Will couldn't have been more surprised if Hardy had set fire to the chuckwagon. "Hardy, if we keep on like we started, they won't be nothin' but hide racks, time we get to Dodge."

Hardy Buckelew didn't bother to argue with him. He just straightened up and gave Will that "I'm the boss around here" look that not even Will would argue with. Hardy rode back to the drags and commenced pushing the slow ones.

From then on, Hardy took over the herd. The first couple of days Will Peril tried every way he could to slow things down. But Hardy would just run over him. Will finally gave up and took a place at swing, his shoulders slumped like he had been demoted to horse wrangler. In a way, I guess you might say he had.

Hardy Buckelew was as hard to get along with on the trail as he had been on the cow hunt—harder, maybe. He was up of a morning before first light, rousing everybody out of bed. "Catch up on your sleep next winter," he would growl. And he wouldn't let the drive stop till it was too dark to see. I remember an afternoon early in the drive when Few Lively set up camp on a nice little creek. It was about six o'clock when the point came even with the place. If Will had been bossing the outfit, right there's where we would have bedded the herd. But Hardy Buckelew rode up to the wagon in a lope, looking like he was fixing to fight somebody.

"What're you doin' here?" he demanded.

Few Lively swallowed about twice, wondering what he had done wrong. "I always camp here. Good water, plenty of grass. Ain't nothin' ahead of us half as good."

Hardy's face was dark with anger. "There's two more hours of good daylight. Now you git that team hitched up and that camp moved a couple more miles up the trail."

As cook, and as one of the old men of the outfit, Few wasn't used to being talked to that way. "There ain't no good water up there, Mister Buckelew."

"We'll drink what there is or do without. Now you git movin'!"

Hardy was like that, day in and day out. He would wear out four or five horses a day just riding back and forth from drag up to the point and back again, stopping every little bit to cuss somebody out and tell him to push them harder. We rode from can-see to can't, Hardy's rough voice never very far away. Not able to fight Hardy Buckelew, and having to work it off someway, some of the boys took to fighting with one another. A couple of them just sneaked off one night while they were on night guard. Didn't ask for their time or anything. Didn't want to face Hardy Buckelew.

Time we got to the Red River, the whole outfit was about ready to bust up. I think if one man had led off, the rest of us would have ridden out behind him, leaving Hardy Buckelew alone with all those steers. Oh, Will Peril probably would have stayed, but nobody else. That's the way it usually is though. Everybody waits for somebody else to start, and nobody does.

Like the year before, it was raining when we got to the Red. The river was running a little bigger than usual as Will Peril rode ahead to take a look at it. He came back and told the point man to keep on going till he reached the other side.

Hardy Buckelew had loped up right after Will Peril and took a long look at the river. He came back holding his hand up in the air, motioning the men to stop.

"We're campin' right here."

Middle of the day, and Hardy Buckelew wanted to camp! We looked at each other like we couldn't believe it, and I think we all agreed on one thing. He'd finally gone crazy.

Will Peril said, "Hardy, that river's just right to cross. Got enough water runnin' to swim them and keep them out of the quicksand. Not enough current to give them much trouble."

Hardy shrugged his shoulders as if he had already said all he wanted to say about it. "We're goin' to camp—rest up these cattle."

Will was getting angry now, his face red and his fists clenched up. "Hardy, it's rainin'. If we don't get them across now, we're liable to have to wait for days."

Hardy just turned and gave him a look that would melt a bar of lead. "This is *my* herd. I say we're goin' to rest these cattle."

And rest them we did, there on the south bank of the Red, with the rain falling and the river beginning to swell. Will Peril would go down by the river and pace awhile, then come back and try arguing again. He had just as well have sat down with the rest of us and kept dry under the big wagonsheet stretched out from the wagon. He couldn't have moved Hardy Buckelew with a team of horses.

We were camped close to Jim Buckelew's grave. Old Hardy rode off down there and spent a while. He came back with his eyes aglow like they had been the fall before, when I had brought him here in the buckboard. He spent little time under the wagonsheet, in the dry. He would stand alone in the rain and stare at that mud-red river.

"He'll catch his death out there," Will Peril muttered, watching the old man like a mother hen watches a chick. But he didn't go out to get him.

The old man had never said a word to anybody about Jim. Still, we knew that was all he was thinking of. We could almost feel Jim right there in camp with us. It was an eerie thing, I'll tell you. I would be glad when we got out of that place.

The second day, after standing by the river a long time, Hardy walked in and spoke to Will Peril. "Is the river the way it was the day Jim drowned?"

Will's eyes were almost closed. "No, I'd say it was a little worse that day."

The old man went out in the rain and watched the river some more. It kept rising. He came back with the same question, and Will gave him the same answer. Now alarm was starting in Will's face.

Finally the old man came back the third time. "Is it as big now as it was that day?"

Will Peril's cheekbones seemed to stand out as the skin drew tight in his whiskered face. "I reckon it is."

The look that came into the old man's gray eyes then was something I never saw before and have never seen

123

again. He turned toward his horse. "All right, boys," he said evenly, "let's go now. We're puttin' them across."

Talk about surprise, most of us stood there with our mouths open like we'd been hit in the head with the flat side of an ax. But not Will Peril. He must have sensed it coming on. He knew the old man better than anybody.

"You've waited too long, Hardy," he said. "Now it can't be done."

"We couldn't go across earlier," spoke Hardy. "We'd have been cheatin' Jimbo. No Buckelew ever started anything but what it got finished. We're goin' to finish this job for *him*." Hardy shoved his left foot in the stirrup and started to swing into the saddle.

Will Peril took three long strides toward him. "Listen to me, Hardy, I'm fixin' to tell it to you straight. Jim rode off into somethin' too big for him and knew it. He was playin' the fool. You've got no call to take it up for him."

Hardy's eyes blazed. If he had had a gun, I think he might have shot Will.

"He was my boy. He was a Buckelew." Hardy's eyes left Will and settled on the rest of us. "How about it, you-all comin'?"

We all just stood there.

Hardy looked us over, one by one. We couldn't meet his eyes. "Then stay here," he said bitterly, pulling himself into the saddle. "I'll do it alone!"

Will Peril was close to him now. Will reached out and grabbed the reins. "Hardy, if you won't stop, I'll stop you!"

"Let go, Will!"

"Get down, Hardy!"

They stared hard at each other, neither man giving ground. All of a sudden the old man swung down and waded into Will.

Will wasn't young, but he was younger than Hardy Buckelew. Most of us thought it would be over with in a hurry. It was, but not the way we expected. Hardy was like a wild man, something driving him as we had never seen him driven before. He took Will by storm. His fists pounded Will like mallets, the sound of them solid and hard, like

124

the strike of an ax against a tree. Will tried, but he couldn't stand up under that. Hardy beat him back, and back, and finally down.

The old man stood over him, swaying as he tried for breath. His hands and face were bloody, his eyes afire. "How about it now?" he asked us again. "You comin'?" When we didn't, he just turned and went back to his horse.

You had to figure him crazy, the way he worked those cattle, getting them started, forcing the first of them off into the water. We stood around like snake-charmed rabbits, watching. We'd picked Will Peril up and dragged him under the wagonsheet, out of the rain. He sat on the muddy ground, shaking his head, his gaze following Hardy Buckelew.

"You tried," I told Will. "You can't blame yourself for what he does now."

Will could see that Hardy was going to take at least a few of those cattle out into the water, with or without us. The trail boss stood up shakily.

"You boys can do what you want to. I'll not let him fight it alone!"

We looked at Will, catching up his horse, then we looked at each other. In a minute we were all on horseback, following.

It was the same as it had been the last time, the water running bankwide and strong. It was a hard fight, just to get those cattle out into the river. They were smarter than us, maybe—they didn't want to go. I don't really know how we did it, but we got it done. Old Hardy Buckelew took the point, and we strung them out.

Time or two there, I saw the leaders begin to drift, and I thought it was over for Hardy the way it had been for Jim. But Hardy Buckelew was fighting, and Will Peril moved up there to help him.

I can't rightly say what the difference was that we made it this time, when we hadn't the time before. Maybe it was the rest the cattle and horses had before they started across. Maybe they were tougher too, the way they had been driven. But mostly I think it was that determined old man up there ahead of us, hollering and swinging his rope and raising hell. He was crazy for going, and we were crazy for following him.

But we made it.

It was a cold and hungry bunch of water-soaked cowboys who threw the herd together on the north bank of the Red. We couldn't get the chuckwagon across—didn't even try—so we went without supper that night and slept without blankets.

But I don't think anybody really minded it much, once it was over. There was the knowledge that we had taken the Red's challenge and made it across. Then too, there was the satisfaction we got out of seeing peace come into Hardy Buckelew's face. We could tell by looking at him that he was one of us again, for the first time in a nearly a year.

Next morning we floated the wagon over and had a chance to fill our bellies with beef and beans and hot coffee.

At Few Lively's fire, Hardy Buckelew looked at Will Peril and said: "From here on, Will, I'm turnin' it back over to you. Run it the way you want to. I'm goin' home."

Surprised, Will said, "Home? Why?"

Hardy Buckelew smiled calmly. "You were right, Will, I'm too old for this foolishness. But I owed a debt for Jimbo. And I'd say that you and me—all the boys in the outfit—have paid it in full."

Relics

The deputy sheriff sat hunched on the wagon tongue, tin plate in his hand, wolfing down cold beef, cold beans, and the morning's biscuits as if he hadn't eaten in a couple of days. Wagon cook George Davenport, standing by the chuckbox, watched dourly as he kneaded sourdough for noon biscuits. He considered how disappointed that kid horse wrangler was going to be in an hour or so when he rode in for his mid-morning snack of cold biscuits and left-over breakfast steak; there wasn't going to be any.

The deputy washed down a big mouthful with black coffee—that was one thing always hot around George's campfire, no matter what time of day it was—and said for the third time at least: "If he should happen along this way, don't you be tryin' to make a hero out of yourself, old-timer. You just give him anything he asks for and then send for us right away. He'd kill you in a minute if you was to give him cause."

George Davenport nodded passively and went on with his work. He wasn't fixing to try to do anything about Enos Foxley if he happened by this chuckwagon, nor would he send for the law. George was going to be sixty years old next October, Lord willing, and one way he had gotten this far was by minding his own business. Over the years he had fed more than one outlaw at his wagon and had given several a bunk in whatever ranch shack, dugout, or tent he happened to be living in at the time. He had never felt an obligation to say anything about it. As long as Enos Foxley did neither him nor the T Bar Cattle Company any harm,

George looked upon him as the law's worry, not his own. He couldn't remember any of the back-trail breed had ever done him any personal injury, something he couldn't say for those jerkwater "laws" that was always looking to lock a man up and fine him his whole month's pay for cutting loose a little.

The deputy went back to the cold Dutch ovens to refill his plate, and finished cleaning out what little he hadn't taken the first time. George looked over east toward the hills; he was expecting the kid to come in from the horse herd just about any time now.

Well, the boy would just have to listen to his stomach growl this morning and hold out till dinner with the rest of the men. It had been so long since George had had that young appetite, he found it hard to remember anymore. One disadvantage of growing old was loss of appetite. Or maybe it was an advantage; he hadn't quite decided which. He had lost his old appetite not only for food but for whisky and women as well. That lent to tranquillity in his downhill years. It also lent to his being able to save a modest nest egg to buy him a little house on the edge of town, where he could live out his time doing something light, like maybe running a ten-by-twelve chili joint. He had begun to fancy that idea lately, especially during the cold winter months just past. The greatest luxury of all would be sleeping until six or maybe even seven o'clock any morning he felt like it. A good wagon cook was never in the blankets past four in the morning. It was getting so his rheumy bones hated to leave that warm bedroll and get up to the black morning chill.

The deputy took the last piece of the last biscuit and wiped his plate clean with it, getting every remnant of the beans. George half expected him to wipe the pot too, but he didn't.

"You got a gun?" the deputy asked.

"You ever see a chuckwagon that didn't have a gun someplace? I keep a pistol in the chuckbox."

"Well, you stay clear of it if Enos Foxley comes along.

He won't give you no chance. You sure you know what he looks like?"

George assured him for the third or fourth time he had seen Foxley around the saloons last winter and would know his hide in a tanyard. "All right," the deputy said, walking toward the horse he had tied much too close to George's wagon, "you remember what I told you; he killed that storekeeper over by Midland for the sixty-seventy dollars in his cashbox. A man like that'll do anything. He comes by here, you let us know."

George was beginning to glower. The deputy was using that patronizing voice people save for kids and old folks; George didn't consider himself either one. He watched the man swing into the saddle and thought quietly he was beginning to run to gut. Seemed like a lot of these town laws had a tendency in that direction. George remembered cooking through spring roundup for the 07's five or six years ago when this same hombre was on the payroll as a cowpuncher. He hadn't been much of a cowboy; he wasn't much of a deputy sheriff either, George judged. He was relieved when the man finally rode through a spring patch of yellow and purple flowers and disappeared over the greening hill to the south, in the general direction of Midland.

George gave one more moment's thought to Enos Foxley, decided the man had probably lit out for Old Mexico, and put him out of his mind. He walked over to the coffeepot and found to his relief that it was still half full; the deputy hadn't been able to drink it all after stuffing himself on the leftover breakfast. George wouldn't have to put any fresh coffee on for a while.

He lost himself in his work, scrubbing up the morning's breakfast ovens and last night's bean pot the deputy had emptied. The dough sat on the hinged-down chuckbox lid, rising for the biscuits he would pinch off later and cook in a Dutch oven, hot coals shoveled over top and under bottom.

Presently he heard a rattle of trace chains. He turned, wondering for a minute what that fool kid Jug was up to.

He saw a hunched figure riding a deep-bodied old farm wagon drawn by a pair of workhorses that had seen better days. Sam Weaver, face hidden by a month's growth of tobacco-stained gray whiskers, waved faintly and drew his team to a halt a respectable distance from George's wagon, where they wouldn't stir dust to drift into George's fixings. That was more thoughtfulness than the deputy had shown.

"Howdy, George," Sam hailed in a voice rough as cedar bark. "Thought I'd stop by and see how you're doin'."

Thought you'd stop by and get some of my cooking instead of fix for yourself, George thought. He wouldn't have said it aloud for fifty dollars in silver. He had known Sam Weaver for too many years.

Sam had a heavy tarp drawn tightly over the wagonbed and tied down so no horse would work its nose under there and eat any of what he carried—grain soaked in a strychnine poison. He looked back to make sure the tarp had in no way worked loose, then stiffly, carefully began to crawl down from the old spring seat. He winced, and George knew Sam's knees hurt him with every step he took. Sam was even older than George, by maybe five or six years. At one time or another during the long years he had worked as a cowboy, he had broken just about every major bone in his body, except perhaps his neck. So, for that matter, had George. But at least George had finally developed some proficiency as a cook, so he could stand off and watch some other poor devil climb up there and do battle with those owl-headed broncs.

Sam had never known anything but punching cows. Now he was too old for that and they had given him the job of running that poison wagon, killing prairie dogs off of the T Bar. A new state law had been passed in Texas, with the concurrence of most landowners, requiring every owner to eradicate prairie dogs from his property or pay an assessment for the state or county government to do it. It had been decided the prairie dog did too much damage to the grasslands and caused too many crippled horses and men. The easiest way to get him was simply to shovel some poisoned grain down the hole in which the prairie dog lived.

It was a job even a worn-out old puncher like Sam Weaver could handle.

Sam had a camp of his own, but he was always hungry when he came by George's wagon. Sam never could boil water without making it taste scorched. "What you got that's good to eat?" he asked as he limped up to George's smouldering fire and looked hopefully at the ovens.

George said testily, "You're too late if you've come to eat. I just fed it all to one of them laws from town."

Sam didn't take his word for it; he poked around all the ovens, lifting the lids off with a long black pothook. When he turned, he was trying to cover his disappointment. "Must've been a hungry one."

No hungrier than Sam, George thought. He felt his impatience ebb. *Hell, I'll be old myself one of these days.* "Get you some coffee and set down someplace. I'll fry you up a strip of beef and a little bread, squaw style."

"I don't want to be no bother," Sam said apologetically. "I was just ridin' by."

George knew he had probably ridden a right smart out of his way. He partially unwrapped a section of tarp from around a quarter of beef hanging off of the chuckbox. He sliced a generous strip of steak. He hoped that kid wrangler didn't ride in here and catch him at it; he would be pestering George every day to do the same thing, and George wasn't about to start any new bad habits. He had enough already.

Sam sat on a big mesquite trunk that George had been using for a woodchopping block. He nursed a tin cup of coffee in his stiff hands. He had a weary look about him— a man who had long since earned the right to sit in the shade but never had been able to afford it. George heated grease in an open Dutch oven, then dropped the steak and a big pinch of bread dough into it. He straightened, pressing his hands against the small of his back where the rheumatism had been getting at him. He looked first at Sam's patient old horses, standing droop-headed in the traces, then at the wagon itself.

"You ever carry anything to eat when you're out workin'?"

"Sometimes, when I think of it. Mainly I just carry me a jug, and a bucket to fix coffee in."

"You ever get scared foolin' with that poison? Ever think what would happen to you if you was to get a little of it mixed up in your food? Just a pinch off of your hands might be enough to—" He broke off. The thought was painful to contemplate.

"I just have to watch what I'm doin'." Sam shrugged. "A man could hurt himself with a wheelbarrow if he didn't watch."

George used a long fork to turn over the steak and the wad of dough. "It ever bother you, Sam, what you're doin' to them poor prairie dogs?" He frowned. "They was here even before *we* was, and *we* been here since they built the mountains and dug the Pecos River."

Sam shrugged again, but George could see he had touched him in a spot that hurt. "Somebody's goin' to do it, George. It's the law. There ain't much anybody'll hire me for anymore. I got to turn my hand at *somethin'*."

"It's goin' to be a different-lookin' country when all them prairie dogs are gone. It won't seem right without them."

"It's the law," Sam said defensively.

George nodded, recognizing the inevitability but saddened by it. The prairie dog was a relic of the past, a relic nobody wanted anymore. They were using another relic, Sam, to get rid of it.

What'll they do to get rid of Sam? he wondered, knowing the answer even as the question crossed his mind. They would simply ignore him, and one day he would be gone.

It probably wouldn't be much longer before they would be trying to ignore George too. But they would play hell doing it. He had money—damn near seven hundred dollars stashed in the Midland bank—and people didn't ignore a man who had money.

George made Sam wash his hands before he would let him start on the steak and fried bread; he was afraid Sam might have some of that strychnine on his fingers. Sam made a good start on the food. George knew that he probably hadn't had anything except coffee since yesterday. He wondered why it was that some old people hated so badly to cook. It beat hell out of riding broncs, or trying to.

The horse wrangler came in when Sam had about half finished eating what George had cooked for him. The boy rode a good stout young sorrel horse the boss had let him break during the slow time last winter and had kindly left in the kid's string. When an outfit let a kid keep a really good horse, that was a sign he was working his way up in the world. The boy called the horse Red, appropriate enough in view of the color. Jug would have stuck both bare feet into a bucket of hot coals rather than let anything happen to that horse.

He was tying the reins to the rear wheel of Sam's wagon when George hollered, "Git that horse away from there! Don't you know that's full of poisoned grain?"

Jug yanked the reins free and walked the horse out to a mesquite tree well away from the wagon.

George grumbled, "Young boys and young horses . . . not a lick of brains in either one of them."

"You got no patience," Sam said, "and no memory either."

Jug Adams walked to the cookfire, whistling expectantly. *Happy as if he had good sense*, George thought. He figured Jug to be about sixteen; Jug claimed twenty. George was dubious about the "Adams" part too. In all likelihood Jug was an East Texas farm boy who had run away from home and didn't want to be found until he had made good on his own, a full-fledged cowboy drawing a grown man's wages and drinking a man's whisky. George had seen fifty like him over the years. Hell, he had *been* one like him a long time ago. He remembered, despite what Sam had said.

Jug found the pans empty and turned to George in dismay. "How come you threw everything out?"

"I didn't. I had company."

Sam Weaver's dull gray eyes brightened as he watched the boy hunt around the chuckbox in vain. He looked down at the plate in his lap, then back to the boy. "Jug, I got more here than I can eat. Come share it with me."

George protested, "He ain't goin' to starve between now and noon." Sam needed the food more than Jug did.

Sam replied, "You're too old and cranky to remember how hungry a boy can get. But I remember. Come on, Jug, finish it so I don't get the bellyache."

When Jug had finished Sam's steak and bread, he gave vent to his curiosity. He had to know who had visited the camp and why. George told him about the deputy and that the laws were all hunting Enos Foxley.

The boy perked up. "I've heard about Foxley. They say he can be a mean one. They got any reward out for him?"

George frowned. It was not healthy for boys to get overly interested in such things; pretty soon they would get to thinking the world was made of easy money and they wouldn't want to sweat anymore. "He didn't mention no reward."

"I'll bet there is one. I sure wish he'd come by here. I could use a little extra cash."

Sam smiled. "What would you do with it, son?"

"I'd buy me a new saddle to put on Red. That's one thing. Then I'd—" He stopped. He had already covered the important part.

George said crustily, "Man like Enos Foxley comes by, you'd better just look off and whistle a tune so you don't see nothin' or hear nothin'. If the laws want him, let the laws find him."

After a bit the young wrangler drifted off toward the scattering remuda, which was his responsibility. It would be his job to take the horses to the morning gather when the cowboys bunched the herd. They would change to fresh mounts. A little after the boy left, Sam decided he had better leave too; he had a prairie dog "town" to work.

"You come back by when you get done," George told him. "I'll see that you have somethin' to eat."

"I'll do that," Sam said, and put his team into an easy trot, jingling the chains as he made his way around the hill.

The cowboys came in at noon, eating by relays so some

of the crew could always be with the cattle herd. It was out of sight to the east, but now and again when the breeze came just right, George could hear the bawling. They were branding the calves, whittling ears, turning prospective bulls into a better prospect for beef.

When the cowboys were all gone and the dishes were washed, George stretched out under the shade of the wagon for the siesta he normally took when he wasn't on the move between camps. The breeze was cool, and it didn't take him long to drop off. He didn't know how long he slept, but when he awoke it was suddenly and with a start. He sat upright, nearly bumping his head on the belly of the wagon.

A man stood by the chuckbox. George couldn't see much of him above the belt buckle, but he saw the six-shooter shoved into the waistband of the striped California-style pants. He first thought it was another of those hungry laws. He crawled stiffly out from under the wagon, taking his time about straightening up because of a nagging pain in his back.

He saw the face then and knew this was no lawman. This was Enos Foxley.

"Didn't go to wake you up," Foxley said. The words were apologetic, but the voice wasn't. The words were merely form, an obligation. George knew if he hadn't awakened by himself, Foxley would have awakened him. Foxley asked, "Could I trouble you for somethin' to eat?"

George told him there was coffee in the pot, but Foxley had already found it. His rummaging for a cup was probably what had brought George out of his nap. "The coffee's fine," Foxley said, "but it ain't enough to carry me far. I'd be obliged if you could let me have somethin' more substantial." The words were polite, but the eyes were commanding and cold.

George told him to help himself to what was in the pots, left over from dinner. He remembered there had been several high-rise biscuits in one Dutch oven, and a pot of beans usually lasted at least two meals. A couple or three strips of steak had been left; he had put them in the oven on top of the bread, knowing Jug would surely come by during the afternoon, and maybe Sam too.

Foxley was nervous in the way he watched George, so George made it a point to stand out in the open, several steps away from him, hoping to demonstrate his own peaceful intentions and set the man's mind at ease. Several of this twisty breed had crossed his trail over the years; he had found it prudent not to cause them anxiety. Most were like a badger—pure hell when they thought they were in a corner.

Thank God, he thought, there weren't many of this kind left. They belonged to another time, and that time was gone. George might grieve a little over the prairie dog or the passing of the open range, but he would feel relief when the last Enos Foxley was gone.

Foxley ate with a hunger that bordered on ferocity. He was even hungrier than that soft-bellied deputy. His gaze stayed on George most of the time but periodically made a long sweep around him, making sure nothing came near that he didn't see. When his worst hunger had been appeased, he slowed a little, taking more time with the second plate. He studied George intently and without trust. "Ain't I seen you before?"

George admitted, "I spent some time in Midland around Christmas."

Foxley's eyes narrowed. "Then I reckon you know who I am?"

George figured a lie would be worse than the truth; it would be too obvious. "I know you."

Foxley held his silence a minute, eating. "I didn't go to kill that storekeeper. Damn fool tried to pull a gun out of a drawer. That made it self-defense, the way I see it."

That the storekeeper had been a damn fool, George had no doubt; the fact that Foxley was robbing him at the time made it difficult for George to accept the notion of self-defense. He chose not to make an issue of it, however.

Foxley finished the plate and went back to the pans.

He couldn't really be hungry anymore, but he was probably going by the old Indian adage that when a man had the chance to eat, he ought to take all his system could absorb; he never knew when the next meal might come to him. The breeze brought the sound of the bawling cow herd, a long way off. Foxley turned his ear to it, listening.

He said, "That horse of mine is about caved in. Which-away's your remuda?"

For the first time George lied to him. "I don't rightly know. The wrangler ain't been in since dinner."

What Foxley had done to a reckless storekeeper a long way from here was none of George's business. But when he contemplated taking a T Bar horse, that was getting too close to home. What's more, that fool kid would probably put up a fuss and get a gun barrel applied over his ear.

Foxley's eyes bored into George; he didn't know whether to believe the cook or not. "Old-timer, I do need me a fresh horse."

George stared silently at him with the best poker face he had.

Foxley turned suddenly, startled, and drew the six-shooter. George heard the trace chains again. Sam Weaver was coming back with his wagon. Foxley glanced urgently at George, his eyes asking.

George said, "It's nobody that'll bother you. It's just old Sam Weaver. The company's got him poisonin' prairie dogs."

Foxley kept his hand on the pistol just the same, until Sam had drawn the team to a halt and was climbing down on the right front wheel, taking his time. He stopped and squinted, trying to get a clear image of Foxley. Sam's eyes were none too good. Either he was too proud to wear glasses or he didn't have the money. George eased out toward him, trying to head him off.

"Sam," he said roughly, "I got nothin' for you to eat. You'd just as well be gettin' back to your own camp."

But Sam Weaver was close enough now for a good look at Foxley. George knew from Sam's eyes that the old man recognized him. The presence of two men in camp would make Foxley more nervous than he already was, even if the two were old.

"Sam," George said, "I ain't got time to mess with you now."

Sam said stubbornly, "You already got company. A little more ain't goin' to hurt you."

George understood then. Sam had the notion George was in danger and that by staying here he might somehow protect him. "Sam . . ." he protested, then ran out of words. There was no use in arguing. Old men like that had a way of being unreasonable.

Enos Foxley took a few steps toward the wagon, his eyes on Sam's horses. George could see him weighing the proposition, then deciding against it. His own horse, even tired, was better than either of Sam's. Foxley shoved the pistol back into his waistband.

George knew he could do nothing now except stand here with Sam and hope Foxley would soon decide it was time to be riding. He thought about the pistol in the chuckbox, but he wouldn't have gone near it for a thousand dollars in gold coin carried to him in silken bags by twelve naked maidens on horseback.

For a minute he thought Foxley was fixing to go. The outlaw walked out to where his horse was tied, then stopped there, looking to the west. George cursed under his breath. "That damn fool kid. I swear, that appetite of his will be the death of him before he has a chance to outgrow it."

Jug Adams came riding in, whistling. He was on Red again; George wondered sometimes if that poor horse ever had a rest. Jug waved at Sam as he rode to the same mesquite where he had tied Red earlier in the day. "Howdy, Sam, you back already? Hope you got ol' George to fix us somethin' fresh to eat."

George wanted to holler at the kid to get the hell out of there, but it wouldn't have been any use. He would have asked "What?" twice and "Why?" afterward.

Jug didn't know Enos Foxley from Abraham Lincoln.

He waved in his thoughtless, friendly way and said, "Hello, friend, you another one of them lawmen?"

George closed his eyes and said some cusswords he hadn't been using much of late.

Foxley said, "No, son, not a law. Just a passin' stranger. Good-lookin' horse you got there."

"Best horse in the whole outfit," Jug said proudly. "I'd stand him up against anything in this country or any of them that adjoins it."

Goddammit, Jug, George thought, *I wisht you'd shut up!*

Foxley said, "I've got a pretty good one here myself, if he wasn't tired out. He'd make a nice swap for that sorrel of yours."

Jug hadn't begun to catch on. "Red's not for tradin'."

Foxley had been walking slowly toward Jug while he talked. He reached out and took Red's reins. "I'm makin' the trade, boy. You'd better stand back over yonder with them friends of yours and be good so I don't have to do anything unpleasant."

Only now did it soak in on Jug that this man intended to take his horse away from him. He grabbed at the reins, gripping them above Foxley's hands, near the bits. "Mister, I don't know who you think you are—"

"You know, if you'll think about it."

Jug thought about it, and George could tell that he finally realized who he was dealing with. But it made no difference. Jug grabbed the reins with both hands and held tight.

"You ain't takin' my horse!"

Foxley glanced toward George as if asking him for help. "Dammit, man, I ain't got time to mess with a fool kid."

George said, "Jug, you'd better come here to me!"

Jug had no such intention. He held bitterly to the reins. Foxley's face darkened. "Oh, hell," he said, and pulled the six-shooter from his waistband.

George's heart went to his throat. He thought Foxley was about to shoot the kid. Foxley swung the barrel and struck Jug a glancing blow to the side of his head. Jug went to his knees, his floppy old felt hat sailing off, but he didn't let loose of the reins for long. He groped and caught them.

"Damned hard-headed kid!" Foxley said angrily, and swung the gun barrel again.

Sam cried, "George, he's killin' that boy!" Sam turned and ran for the chuckwagon.

George called, "Sam . . ."

Nothing he could have done would have stopped what happened. Sam reached into the chuckbox and came up with the pistol George kept there. But he didn't know that George always kept a chamber empty to avoid an accident. Sam brought the pistol around and trained it on Foxley.

George heard the click of the hammer falling on a spent cartridge, then heard the roar of Foxley's six-shooter. Sam Weaver slammed back against the wagon wheel, then went down like he had been struck by a sledgehammer. He never moved.

Jug lay on his stomach, his head bleeding. He was trying to crawl but getting nowhere.

"What about you, old man?" Foxley demanded of George. "Am I goin' to have trouble with you too?"

George pulled his eyes away from Sam, shuddering from a hard and sudden chill. "No trouble."

"Worst bunch of damn fools I ever come up against," Foxley complained. "I didn't come here to kill anybody. I just come for somethin' to eat and a horse. I'm takin' the sorrel."

Frozen, George stood watching him. He fought an urge to turn and look again at Sam. He knew it was useless to try to help. Sam was dead.

Foxley swung into Jug's saddle, tried the stirrups, and stepped down again. "Too short for me. I'm goin' to change my saddle onto him. You put some food into a sack, old man, so I'll have somethin' to eat along the way."

George couldn't seem to move his feet. Foxley waved the six-shooter at him. "I'll tell you just one more time. Get me some food to take along."

George found his feet and turned toward the wagon.

* * *

The sheriff was older than his deputy and assumed none of the younger man's superior airs. He was strictly business as he lifted the blanket back over the bearded face of old Sam.

George sat hunched on a bedroll, chilled and numb, as if he had been kicked in the stomach. He studied the kid lying on a blanket beneath the wagon, stirring a little but not rising up. Jug hadn't been clear in his head yet; he didn't remember what had happened to him. He would have time later to remember, a whole lifetime.

The deputy said defensively, "I told them, Joe; I told them not to mess around with Foxley. I told them to leave him to us."

The sheriff cut him a sharp, quick look that told him to shut the hell up. He turned back to George with sympathy in his eyes. "I'm sorry about old Sam. And I'm sorry about the long head start Foxley got on us. Three hours . . . we'll never make that up."

George hadn't said much; he hadn't felt like it. He had given short answers to direct questions, and that was all. He shook his head. "You can catch up to him all right. All you got to do is to follow that sorrel's tracks."

"We been pushin' our horses hard. His is probably fresher."

"Won't matter," George said flatly. "Sooner or later he'll stop to eat what I packed for him. That's where you'll find him."

The sheriff's eyes narrowed, asking a question. George said, "I put the food in a sack out of Sam's wagon."

The impact hit the sheriff like a fist. "My God! You poisoned him!"

George shrugged, looking back at Jug Adams and Sam.

The sheriff hurriedly swung into his saddle and motioned for the deputy to follow him. They rode out of camp in a long trot, following Foxley's tracks. The sheriff was saying maybe if they hurried they would get to Foxley before he stopped to eat. But they wouldn't, George knew.

The T Bar wagonboss stood slack-jawed, staring at

George in disbelief. George explained, "He killed Sam. Sam's poison has killed *him*, or will. Seems right enough to me."

"But he's a man, George."

George shook his head again. "He's a relic." He stared at the blanket that covered Sam Weaver. His voice was cold. "Who's got time or use for relics anymore?"

Uncle Jeff and the Gunfighter

Out in West Texas the old-timers still speak occasionally of the time my uncle Jeff Barclay scared off the gunfighter Tobe Farrington. It's a good story, as far as it goes, but the way they tell it doesn't quite go far enough. And the reason is that my father was the only man who ever knew the whole truth. Papa would have carried the secret to the grave with him if he hadn't taken a notion to tell me about it a little while before he died. Now that he's buried beside Mother in the family plot over at Marfa, I reckon it won't hurt to clear up the whole story, once and for all.

Papa was the elder of the two brothers. He and Uncle Jeff were what they used to call four-sectioners a long time ago.

Lots of people don't understand about Texas homesteads. When Texas joined the union it was a free republic, with a whopper of a debt. Texas kept title to its land because the United States didn't want to take on all that indebtedness. So in later years Texas had a different homestead law than the other states. By the time Papa and Uncle Jeff were grown, the state of Texas was betting four sections of land against a man's filing fee, his hope, and his sweat that he would starve to death before he proved up his claim. It's no secret that the state won a lot of those bets.

But it didn't win against Papa and Uncle Jeff. They proved up their land and got the title.

Trouble was, their claims were on pasture that old Port

Hubbard had ranched for a long time, leasing from the state. It didn't set well with him at all, because he was used to having people ask him things, not tell him. And there was a reckless streak in Uncle Jeff that caused him to glory in telling people how the two of them had thumbed their noses at Port Hubbard and gotten away with it.

It would be better if I told you a little about Uncle Jeff, so you'll know how it was with him. I've still got an old picture—yellowed now—that he and Papa had taken the day they got title to their four sections apiece, a little more than seventeen hundred acres the way people figure it in most other places. It shows Papa dressed in a plain suit that looks like he had slept in it, and he wears an ordinary sort of wide-brimmed hat set square on his head. But Uncle Jeff has on a pair of those striped California pants they used to wear, and sleeve garters, and a candy-striped shirt. He's wearing one of those huge cowboy hats that went out of style years ago, the ones you could really call ten-gallon without exaggerating much. The hat is cocked over to one side of his head. A six-shooter sits high on his right hip. The clothes make him look like he's on his way to a dance, but the challenge in his eyes makes him look like he's waiting for a fight. With Uncle Jeff, it could have been either one or both.

A lot of ranchers like Port Hubbard made good use of the Texas homestead law. They got their cowboys to file on land that lay inside their ranches. These cowboys would prove up the land, then sell it to the man they worked for. Plenty of cowboys in those days weren't interested in being landowners anyhow, and in a lot of West Texas four sections wasn't enough land for a man to make a living on. It wouldn't carry enough cattle. And farming that dry country was a chancy business, sure enough.

It bothered Hubbard when Papa and Uncle Jeff took eight sections out of his Rocking H ranch. But he held off, figuring they would starve out and turn it back. And meanwhile, they would be improving it for him. When that didn't work the way he expected, he tried to buy it from them. They wouldn't sell.

Hubbard might still have swallowed the loss and gone about his business if Uncle Jeff hadn't been inclined to brag so much.

"He's buffaloed people in this part of the country for twenty years," Uncle Jeff would say, and he didn't care who heard or repeated it. "But we stopped him. He's scared to lay a finger on us."

Papa always felt Port Hubbard wouldn't have done anything if Uncle Jeff hadn't kept jabbing the knife point at him, so to speak. But Hubbard was a proud man, and proud men don't sit around and listen to that kind of talk forever, especially old-time cowmen like Port Hubbard. So by and by Tobe Farrington showed up.

Nobody ever did prove that Port Hubbard sent for him, but nobody ever doubted it. Farrington put in for four sections of land that lay right next to Papa's and Uncle Jeff's. It was on Rocking H country that had been taken up once by a Hubbard cowboy who later got too much whisky over in Pecos and took a fatal dose of indigestion on three .45 slugs.

Everybody in West Texas knew of Tobe Farrington in those days. He wasn't famous in the way of John Wesley Hardin or Bill Longley, but in the country from San Saba to the Pecos River he had a hard name. Folks tried to give him plenty of air. It was known that several men had gone to glory with his bullets in them.

A lot of folks expected to see Farrington just ride over and shoot Papa and Uncle Jeff down, but he didn't work that way. He must have figured on letting his reputation do the job without him having to waste any powder. Papa said it seemed like just about every time he and Uncle Jeff looked up, they would see Tobe Farrington sitting there on his horse, just watching them. He seldom ever spoke, he just looked at them. Papa admitted that those hard gray eyes always put a chunk of ice in the pit of his stomach. But Uncle Jeff wasn't bothered. He seemed to thrive on that kind of pressure.

I didn't tell you that Uncle Jeff had been a deputy once. The Pecos County sheriff had hired him late one

spring, mostly to run errands for him. In those days the
sheriff was usually a tax assessor too. The job didn't last
long. That summer the sheriff got beaten in the primary
election. The next one had needy kinfolks and didn't keep
Uncle Jeff on.

But by that time Uncle Jeff had gotten the feel of the
six-shooter on his hip, and he liked it. What's more, he got
to be a good shot. He liked to ride along and pot jackrabbits
with his pistol. Two or three times this trick got him thrown
off of a boogered horse, but Uncle Jeff would still do it when
he took the notion. That was his way. Nothing ever scared
him much, and nothing ever kept him from doing as he
damn well pleased. Nothing but Papa.

If Tobe Farrington figured his being there was going
to scare the Barclay brothers out of the country, he was
disappointed. So he began to change his tactics. Farrington
had a little bunch of Rocking H cattle with a "vented" brand,
which he claimed he had bought from Hubbard but which
everybody said Hubbard had just loaned him to make the
homestead look legal. He started pushing his cattle over
onto the Barclay land. He didn't do it sneaky. He would
open the wire gates, bold as brass, push the cattle through,
then ride on in and watch them eat Barclay grass. It wasn't
the rainiest country in the world. There was just enough
grass for the Barclay cattle, and sometimes not even that
much.

Uncle Jeff was all for a fight. He wanted to shoot Farrington's cattle. Papa, on the other hand, believed in being
firm but not suicidal. He left his gun at home, took his
horse, and pushed the cattle back through the gate while
Farrington sat and watched.

"He couldn't shoot me," Papa said, "because I didn't
have a gun. He couldn't afford a plain case of murder. When
Farrington killed somebody, he made it a point to be within
the law."

Farrington gave up that stunt after two or three times
because Papa always handled it in the same way.

After that it was little things. Steer roping was a popular
sport in those days. Farrington always rode across Papa's

land to go to Fort Stockton, and while passing through he would practice roping Barclay cattle. It was a rough sport. Throwing down those grown cattle was an easy way to break horns, and often it broke legs as well. Farrington made it a point to break legs.

Uncle Jeff wanted to take a gun and call for a showdown. Papa wouldn't let him. Instead, Papa wrote up a bill for the broken-legged cattle they had had to kill and got the sheriff to go with him to collect. The sheriff was as nervous as a sheepherder at a cowboy convention, but Papa collected.

"Guns are his business," Papa tried to tell Uncle Jeff. "The average man can't stand up against a feller like Tobe Farrington any more than a big-city bookkeeper could ride one of Port Hubbard's broncs. You leave your guns at home or one of these days Farrington'll sucker you into using them. Second prize in his kind of shootin' match is a wooden box."

I reckon before I go any further I ought to tell you about Delia Larrabee. Papa might have been a little prejudiced, but he always said she was the prettiest girl in the country in those days. Uncle Jeff must have agreed with him. Papa met her first and was using all the old-fashioned cowboy salesmanship he had. But Uncle Jeff was a better salesman. It hurt, but when Papa saw how things were, he backed off and gave up the field to Uncle Jeff. Looking at that old picture again, it's not hard to see why Delia Larrabee or any other girl might have been drawn to my uncle. He was quite the young blade, as they used to say.

Tobe Farrington had drawn a joker from the deck every time he tried to provoke a fight with Papa or Uncle Jeff. Stealing grass or injuring cattle hadn't done it. But when he found out about Delia Larrabee and Uncle Jeff, he must have realized he had found the way. The big dance in Fort Stockton gave him his chance.

Papa didn't go that night, or he might have found a way to stop the thing before it went as far as it did. But it still hurt him too much to be around Delia Larrabee, knowing he had lost her. And he hadn't seen any other girl he felt comfortable with. Besides, he was tired because for two days he had been out with a saddle gun, trying to track down a calf-killing wolf. So he let Uncle Jeff go to town alone, though he made sure my uncle left his gun at home.

Tobe Farrington waited around till the dance had been on a good while. That way, when he did show up he would get more attention. And get it he did. Folks said the hall fell almost dead silent when Farrington walked in. Dancers all stopped. Everything stopped but the old fiddler, and his eyes were so bad he couldn't tell a horse from a cow at forty feet. Farrington just stood there till he spotted Uncle Jeff over by the punch bowl. Then he saw Delia Larrabee sitting at the south wall, waiting for Uncle Jeff to fetch her some punch. Farrington walked over, bowed, and said, "You're the prettiest girl in the crowd. I believe I'll have this dance."

Uncle Jeff came hurrying back. He had his fists clenched, but Delia Larrabee shook her head at him to make him stop. She stood up right quick and held out her hands as a sign to Farrington that she wanted to dance with him. She knew what Farrington really wanted. To refuse him would have meant a fight.

But Farrington didn't mean to be stopped. When that tune ended, he kept hold of her hand and forced her into another dance. Uncle Jeff took a step or two forward, like he was going to interfere, but she waved him off. That dance finally ended, but Farrington didn't let her go. When the fiddle started, he began dancing with her again.

Uncle Jeff had had enough. He hollered at the fiddler to stop the music.

By that time nobody was dancing but Farrington and Delia Larrabee anyway. Everybody else had pulled back, waiting.

Uncle Jeff walked up to Farrington with his face red. "Turn her loose."

Farrington gripped her fingers a little tighter. "This is too pretty a gal to waste her time with a little greasy-sack rancher like you. I'm takin' over."

Uncle Jeff's picture shows that he had a powerful set

of shoulders. When he swung his fist on somebody, it left a mark. Tobe Farrington landed flat on his back. By instinct he dropped his hand to his hip. But he had had to check his pistol at the door, same as everybody else. With a crooked grin that spelled murder, he pushed to his feet.

Delia Larrabee had her arms around Uncle Jeff and was trying to hold him back. "Jeff, he means to kill you!"

Uncle Jeff put her aside and looked Tobe Farrington in the eye. "I left my gun at home."

Farrington said flatly, "You could go and get it."

"All right. I will."

Farrington frowned. "On second thought, Barclay, it'd still be nighttime when you got back. Night's a poor time for good shootin'. So I tell you what: I'm goin' home. Tomorrow afternoon I'll come back to town. Say at five o'clock. If you still feel like you got guts enough, you can meet me on the street. We'll finish this right." His eyes narrowed. "But if you decide *not* to meet me, you better clear out of this country. I'll be lookin' around for you."

They were near the door, where the guns were checked. Farrington took his, strapped the belt around his waist, then drew the pistol. "So there's no misunderstandin', Barclay, I want you to see what I can do."

Thirty feet across the dance hall was a cardboard notice with the words FORT STOCKTON. Farrington brought up the pistol, fired once, and put a bullet hole through the first O. Women screamed as the shot thundered and echoed.

Uncle Jeff waited a few seconds, till the thick smoke cleared. "Let me see that thing a minute." Farrington hesitated, then handed it to him. Uncle Jeff fired twice and put holes through the other two O's.

Folks always said afterward that Farrington looked as if he had swallowed a cud of chewing tobacco. He hadn't realized Uncle Jeff was that good.

Uncle Jeff said, "*I'll* be here. Just be sure *you* show up." Right then he would have taken on Wild Bill Hickok.

He didn't go home that night. He knew Papa would argue and plead with him, and he didn't want to listen. He stayed in town with friends. Next morning he was out on the open prairie beyond Comanche Springs, practicing with a borrowed pistol.

Delia Larrabee had tried awhile to reason with him. She told him she would go anywhere with him—California, Mexico—if he would just go, and do it right now. But Uncle Jeff had his mind made up. He would have done this a long time ago if it hadn't been for Papa. So Delia got her father to take her out in a buckboard in the dark hours of early morning to tell Papa what had happened.

"You've got to do something," she cried. "You're the only one who can talk to Jeff."

Papa studied about it a long time. But he knew Uncle Jeff. The only way Papa would be able to stop him now would be to hog-tie him. And he couldn't keep him tied forever.

"I'll try to think of something," Papa promised, "but I doubt that anything will stop it now. You'd best go on home." There was a sadness about him, almost a giving up.

He sat at his table a long time, sipping black coffee and watching the morning sun start to climb. It came to him that Farrington was only doing a job for Port Hubbard, and all that Port Hubbard really wanted was to see the Barclay brothers leave the country. If it came to that, Papa had rather have had Uncle Jeff alive than to own the best eight sections in Pecos County.

He knew Jeff wouldn't listen to him. But maybe Farrington would.

Papa saddled up and started for the frame shack on Farrington's four sections. He still had the saddle gun he had used for hunting the wolf. He didn't really intend to use it. But there was always a chance Farrington might decide to make a clean sweep of the Barclay brothers while he was at it.

Not all the wolves had four legs.

Farrington's shack had originally been a line camp for Hubbard on land inside Papa's claim. When Papa took up the land, Hubbard had jacked up the little house and hauled it out on two wagons. The only thing left at the old campsite was a ruined cistern, surrounded by a little fence to keep stock from falling in. Papa had always intended to come over and fill it up, when he had time.

Now, he thought, *there won't be any need to fill it up. It'll be Hubbard's again.*

He saw smoke curling upward from the tin chimney, and he knew Farrington was at home. "Farrington," Papa called, "it's me, Henry Barclay. I've come to talk to you."

Farrington was slow about showing himself, and he came out wearing his gun. Distrust showed all over him. His hand was close to his gun butt, and it went even closer when Papa's horse turned so that Farrington saw the saddle gun.

"It's past talkin' now, Barclay. There was a time we could've worked this out, but not anymore."

"We still could," Papa said. "What if we give you what Hubbard wants? What if we sell our land to him and clear out?"

Farrington frowned. "Why should I care what Hubbard wants?"

"We don't have to play games, Farrington. I know what you came for, and you know I know it. So now you've won. Leave my brother alone."

"You're speakin' for yourself. But your brother may not see it your way."

"He will, even if I have to tie him up and haul him clear to California in a wagon."

Farrington considered awhile. "You make sense, up to a point. Pity you couldn't have done this a long while back, before I had spent so much time here. Now you might say I got an investment made. What suits Port Hubbard might not be enough to suit *me* anymore."

"You want money? All right, I'll split with you. Half of what Hubbard gives for the land. Only, I don't want Jeff hurt."

"Half of what Hubbard'll give now ain't very much."

"All of it, then. We didn't have anything when we came here. I reckon we could start with nothin' again."

A dry and awful smile broke across Farrington's face. "No deal. I just wanted to see how far you'd crawl. Now I know."

"You're really goin' to kill him?"

"Like I'd kill a beef! And then I'll come and put you off of the land, Barclay. It won't cost Hubbard a cent. You'll sign those papers and drag out of here with nothin' but the clothes on your back!"

That was it, then. Papa turned his horse and made like he was going to ride off. But he knew he couldn't leave it this way. Uncle Jeff was as good as dead. For that matter, so was Papa, for he had no intention of leaving his land if Uncle Jeff died.

Seventy feet from the house, Papa leaned forward as if he was going to put spurs to the horse. Instead, he took hold of the saddle gun and yanked it up out of the scabbard.

Farrington saw what was coming. He drew his pistol and fired just as the saddle gun came clear. But Papa was pulling his horse around. The bullet went shy.

Papa dropped to the ground, flat on his belly. He had lessened the odds by getting distance between him and Farrington. This was a long shot for a pistol. It was just right for Papa's short rifle. Farrington knew it too. He came running, firing as he moved, trying to keep Papa's head down till he could get close enough for a really good shot.

Papa didn't let him get that close. He sighted quick and squeezed the trigger.

Papa had shot a lot of lobo wolves in his day, and some of them on the run. Farrington rolled like one of those wolves. His body twitched a few times, then he was dead.

Papa had never killed a man before, and he never killed one again. He knew it was something he had had to do to save Uncle Jeff. But still he was sick at his stomach. All that coffee he had drunk came up. Later, when he had settled a little, he began wondering how he was going to tell this. Uncle Jeff probably never would forgive him, for he had wanted Farrington for himself. Papa would never be able to convince him Farrington would have killed him. Hubbard would scream *murder*, and it might be hard to convince a jury that it hadn't been just that. Men had been known to murder for much less than a brother's life.

Then it came to him: why tell anybody at all?

Nobody had seen it. For all anyone needed to know, Farrington had just saddled up and ridden away. Gunfighters did that sometimes. Many a noted outlaw had simply disappeared, never to be heard of again. A new country, a new name, a new start . . .

Farrington's horse was in the corral. Actually, it was a Rocking H sorrel of Port Hubbard's. Papa put Farrington's bridle and saddle on him, then hoisted Farrington's body up over the saddle. The horse danced around, smelling blood, and it was a hard job, but Papa got the body lashed down. He went into the house. He took a skillet, a coffee pot, some food—the things Farrington would logically have carried away with him if he were leaving the country. He rolled these up in Farrington's blankets and took them with him.

He worried some over the tracks, and he paused to kick dirt over the patch of blood where Farrington had fallen. But in the north, clouds were building. Maybe it would rain and wash out the tracks. If it didn't rain, at least the wind would blow. In this country, wind could reduce tracks about as well as a rain.

Papa led the sorrel horse with its load out across the Farrington claim and prayed he wouldn't run into any Rocking H cowboys. He stayed clear of the road. When he reached his own land, he cut across to the one-time Hubbard line camp. There he dragged Farrington's body to the edge of the old cistern and dropped him in. He dropped saddle, blankets, and everything else in after him. Then he led the sorrel horse back and turned him loose in Hubbard's big pasture.

Papa was not normally a drinking man, but that afternoon he took a bottle out of the kitchen cabinet and sat on the porch and got drunk.

Late that night, Uncle Jeff came home. He had been drinking too, but for a different reason. He had a couple of friends with him, helping him celebrate.

"Howdy do, big brother," he shouted all the way from the front gate. "It's me, little old Jeff, the livest little old Jeff you ever did see!" He swayed up onto the porch and saw Papa sitting there. "Bet you thought they'd be bringin' me home in a box. You just been sittin' here a-drinkin' by yourself and dreadin' seein' them come. But I'm here, and I'm still a-kickin'. I won. Farrington never showed up."

Papa couldn't make much of a display. "You don't say!"

"I *do* say! The whole town was waitin'. He never came. He was scared of me. Tobe Farrington was scared of *me*!"

Papa said, "I'm glad, Jeff. I'm real glad." He pushed himself to his feet and staggered off to bed.

Next day there must have been thirty people by at one time or another, all wanting to congratulate Jeff Barclay. They didn't see Papa though. He had gone off to fill up that old cistern before a cow fell in it.

It was told all over West Texas how Jeff Barclay, a greasy-sack rancher, had scared Tobe Farrington into backing down. Folks decided Farrington was reputation and nothing else. They always wondered where he went, because nobody ever heard of him after that. Talk was that he had gone into Mexico and had changed his name, ashamed to face up to people after backing down to Jeff Barclay.

Papa was more than glad to let them believe that. Like I said, he kept the secret till just before he died. But it must always have troubled him, and when finally he knew his time was coming, he told me. He kept telling me it was something he hadn't wanted to do but had to because of Uncle Jeff.

The irony was that it didn't really save Uncle Jeff. If anything, it killed him. Being the way he was, Uncle Jeff let the notoriety go to his head. Got so he was always looking for another Tobe Farrington. He turned cocky and quarrelsome. Gradually he alienated his friends. He even lost Delia Larrabee. The only person he didn't lose was Papa.

Papa wasn't there to help him the day Uncle Jeff finally met a man who was like Tobe Farrington. Uncle Jeff was still clawing for his pistol when he fell with two bullets in his heart.

Uncle Jeff's four sections went to Papa, but he sold them along with his own—but not to Port Hubbard. He bought a ranch farther west, in the Davis Mountains.

And Delia Larrabee? She married Papa. I was the oldest of their six sons.

O'Malley's Wife

Larkin O'Malley had a streak of recklessness in him a yard-and-a-half wide. He must have, to have stood in front of a shotgun held by Mary Donovan's father and tell him flat out that he was going to marry her whether the scowling old Irishman liked it or not.

Old Michael Donovan had the hard head of a freighter's mule. But he had grudgingly lowered the shotgun, knowing that this young Texas sheepman was as stubborn as himself, and that he couldn't shoot him.

"She'll leave you," old Donovan had warned darkly. "Mary is a town-raised girl, and she'll not long stand for the sheepherder's life you're taking her to. I'll give your marriage six months. Three months if she's as smart as I know she is."

But Larkin O'Malley had seen the strength of Donovan in the face of his daughter, and he had been confident she could make the change to his kind of life. He had almost forgotten the old man's warning in the rosy glow of the honeymoon.

Now, with the blistering heat of the summer sun heavy upon him, he was plodding along on horseback in the low-hanging gray dust behind a band of black-top merino ewes with their leggy March lambs. And the words kept coming back to him.

"She'll leave you. She'll leave you."

He remembered them each time he saw Mary trying vainly to brush away the clinging dust, or blinking her burning blue eyes against the fiery bite of mesquite smoke

156

from an open campfire, or scrubbing her town-bought clothing by hand on the banks of every half-muddied waterhole
they came to, until the color was faded and the fabric was
beginning to unravel.

Four days west of San Angelo came the first hint of
new trouble. Helping Mary pull the wagon around for evening camp, O'Malley saw two bands of someone else's sheep
ahead, moving eastward toward him—east, when they should
be drifting west. Gently he touched Mary's sun-blistered
hand.

"I'll be back," he said, and swung into the saddle.

He spurred into a long trot, going past his own band
of sheep and reining up near the next band he came to. He
found these sheep gaunt and dragging. So was the bent,
bewhiskered old man who owned them.

The old-timer licked his dry lips to soften them before
he spoke, and his prune-wrinkled face squinched up at the
bitter taste of the dust. "You'd better turn back," he said.
"There hasn't been rain out yonder in six months. There
isn't a drop of water in fifty miles, except for the river. And
Hodge Guyman has that."

Larkin O'Malley frowned, feeling a tug of sympathy
for the old man and his suffering sheep, and thinking of his
own. A few more days of this and they would look as bad.

"I can't turn back now. I'm taking them to the Howard's
Draw country."

"So was I, but you can't get through this way. Guyman
wouldn't leave enough of your sheep for a mutton stew.
Me, I'm going back to San Angelo and drift south. Maybe
I'll work into the Howard's Draw country from somewhere
below."

O'Malley stiffened, looking westward into the slowly
shifting dust. "That could take all summer."

The old man shrugged. "Time doesn't mean much to
a sheep." He edged his horse on and started turning his
flock so it would not mix with O'Malley's.

O'Malley worriedly rubbed the back of his sun-browned
neck and looked up into the hot, dry sky. The sun bore
down relentlessly, the heat waves rippling across the rolling

scrub mesquite and greasewood land. Three dancing whirl-winds boiled up dust at one time, two to the west, one east of him. There was still a fair turf of short grass. Though the long dry spell had left it brittle and brown, sheep could survive on it, provided they had water.

Mary had already shoveled out a pit and kindled a mesquite fire when O'Malley returned to camp and pre-pared to unsaddle. Watching this lithe girl he had married, as the lowering sun picked up a glint of red from her hair, he felt a warmth start inside him.

She had not seen him. She was too busy trying to chop down a half-dead mesquite tree for firewood. It had just enough greenness left to yield each time the ax struck it, then it would spring back. In a surge of Irish temper she swung extra hard. A branch whipped out and struck her. The thorns bit into her arm. She dropped to one knee, letting go the ax.

O'Malley rushed to kneel beside her, gripping her arms. "Did it hurt you, Mary?"

Her pretty lips were cracked from the sun and wind. They pulled tight as she shook her head. "It didn't hurt me. Just made me mad, that's all—mad and disgusted. I'm sick of this bouncy old wagon, sick of cooking over a camp-fire, sick of eating dust. Will we ever get there, Larkin?"

She tried to hold back tears, but one cut a trail down through the thick layer of dust on her comely face. He took her grimy hand and kissed it, and felt the calluses rough against his lips. It was not like the hand he had held when they had stood before the priest during the wedding cer-emony.

"It won't be much longer now, will it, darling?" Mary asked, a note of desperation in her voice.

He looked westward toward the Guyman range and knew there was no choice for him. He shook his head and kissed her. "No, Mary, it won't be long now."

They came to the river late the next day, and he knew they were on Guyman's Two Bar range. He remembered Hodge Guyman well, for once—before he had saved his money and bought his sheep—O'Malley had worked on a ranch above San Angelo where Guyman had moved a herd of cattle through. He had not asked permission, nor had he given any thanks. He had picked the best grass and the best water and had shoved the owner's cattle aside. He had taken what he wanted and had gone on as if it were no more than his due, for he was the son of old Colonel Tom, who had come here in the day of the Comanches and had built an empire of rawhide and steel.

No one had ever dared cross the father, and now no one crossed the son. How could O'Malley cross him now —just himself, a woman, and one old Mexican sheepherder as peaceful as a collie dog?

O'Malley eased his horse down the wide slant of the riverbank beneath the deep spreading shade of huge old native pecan trees. He saw that the river was barely running. Where in normal times the water was thirty or forty feet wide, there were now only sand and gravel bars, and green grass poking up through the hardening mud. Occasional potholes still held water, but the actual running stream was in most places only a step or two wide, and inches deep.

Suddenly O'Malley thought he saw a way. It was a chance, at least, if a man had luck and guts enough to bluff his way through. "Julio!" he called, waving his grease-spotted hat at his herder. "Take the sheep down into the riverbed."

The riverbed wandered crookedly across the range in a generally east-west direction. Following it westward, against the flow, O'Malley could keep his sheep on water for some thirty miles. Beyond that he would have twenty or so of dry, waterless range to cross before he reached the Howard country and home. But sheep were dry-weather animals; they could survive that last twenty miles.

The hard part would be this first thirty.

By the end of the second day he began to hope he was going to get by without being discovered. Up ahead, old Julio occasionally trotted forward afoot to throw rocks at Guyman's cattle so they would leave the river and not mix up with the sheep. There was no sign of any Two Bar men.

But early the afternoon of the third day, trouble came. A cowboy rode down over the edge of the riverbank and reined up sharply, staring in disbelief. With firm purpose he started his horse toward Julio, then saw O'Malley and turned back to meet him. The cowboy was a kid, perhaps eighteen or nineteen, the soft fuzz on his face just beginning to show a dark whisper here and there.

With all the ingrained haughtiness a cowboy could muster against his inferiors, he thrust his jaw forward. "How did you get here, sheepherder?"

O'Malley sat rigidly in the saddle, not yielding an inch. "Straight up the river."

"Hasn't anybody told you this is Two Bar range?"

"I've heard."

The young cowboy stared incredulously, as if O'Malley was by far the most stupid pilgrim he had ever met. "Then, mister, you're asking for it." He pulled his horse around and roughly spurred him up the steepest part of the riverbank.

O'Malley watched him a moment, then drew a slow breath and let his shoulders slump. It wouldn't be long now. He glanced down at his saddle gun, glad for its reassuring feel beneath his leg.

Three hours later the cowboy was back, with company. Six riders slid their horses down the riverbank, almost overrunning some of the startled sheep. One of the men glared at the ewes and lambs as if he were about to tear them apart with his hands. Then his knife-sharp gaze pivoted to O'Malley.

"You're fixing to lose a flock of sheep!"

This was Hodge Guyman. O'Malley remembered him. Young, not over thirty, he was notoriously hot-headed, strong-willed, overbearing. He never forgot or let anyone else forget he was the colonel's son. He tried to carry himself with the stiff pride of an aristocrat, but somehow, to O'Malley, he looked more like a hill-country sheep thief.

O'Malley could see the outraged pride in Guyman's dark eyes and knew the urge that made the young man's hand drop to the butt of the .44 in a hand-tooled holster at his hip. O'Malley reached down and eased up his saddle gun, leisurely laying it across the saddle before him. The muzzle pointed at Guyman.

"You might have time to shoot *one* sheep," he said flatly.

Color flowed into Guyman's face at this unexpected defiance. He glanced quickly at a gray-haired, thin-shouldered rider beside him, his eyes asking. The son of Colonel Tom was begging for advice.

The man said quietly, "Go easy, Hodge. He's liable to kill you."

Guyman's hands cupped over the saddle horn, away from mischief. He slumped a little. But his eyes glowed like those of a caught wolf at the end of a trap chain.

Once, years ago, O'Malley had seen Colonel Tom Guyman angry, and it had been a sight to remember. It struck O'Malley that there was little of the colonel about the son except for what the younger man had consciously copied. Here was all of the arrogance, all of the fire—but none of the judgment. That could be a dangerous shortcoming.

Guyman said, "You don't really think you can get away with it, do you, sheepherder? If six men aren't enough to run these sheep out of here, I can get twelve. If twelve aren't enough, I can get twenty."

There wouldn't be any use talking to him about the dry water holes. It was foolish to try and reason with him about O'Malley's need to get to his home range as quickly as he could. Guyman just wouldn't care.

So O'Malley simply said, "I'm not on your land."

That shook Guyman. He turned his head a little, as if unsure he had heard right. "What do you mean, not on my land? It's *all* my land, a hard day's ride in any direction."

O'Malley shook his head. "All but the riverbed. That belongs to the state of Texas."

Guyman blinked, started to reply, then stopped. Glancing at the older man beside him, he jerked his head back toward O'Malley. His hand inched toward the .44.

The graying rider leaned across and caught his hand. "Hold on, Hodge. He still has that gun. And what's more,

I have a notion he's right. This riverbed belongs to the state. They all do."

Guyman swore. His horse sensed the tension and began fidgeting. Hand flexing in rage, Guyman jerked savagely on the reins. "State or no state, no greasy sheepherder is making a monkey out of me. I'll kill him and his sheep both!"

An edge of impatience arose in the graying rider's face too, the slow anger of the tutor who must keep discipline but is not allowed to punish the master's brats. "Use your head, Hodge, like the colonel would have done. That new sheriff's been itching for you to make a mistake."

This cooled Guyman down some. But in stubborn resentment he said, "The Two Bar used to tell the sheriff what to do."

In the old puncher's face O'Malley could see the faintest trace of contempt. "Your father was still living then."

Hodge Guyman took the full implication, the unstated comparison, and made no reply. But the anger deepened in his eyes. "All right, Newt, what can I do? If I let him get away with this, the whole country'll be thinking the Two Bar can be taken. They'll be down on us like a pack of wolves."

The old rider, Newt, shook his head. "I'm no lawyer, but I'd say there's not much you *can* do, as long as he stays in the riverbed."

It was then that Mary pulled the wagon up to the river's edge to look down and determine what was wrong. Guyman stared at her, the corners of his mouth lifting a little, like the grin of a coyote. Guyman liked women. From Del Rio to Fort Worth, they could tell you about this woman or the other, and Hodge Guyman. He got around. He looked at Mary, and his tone changed.

"Have it your way then, Newt. He can drive his sheep on state property, but we'll escort him. Any sheep that steps up over the bank, we'll shoot."

O'Malley did not like what he saw building in Guyman's eyes as he looked at Mary.

"And get that wagon down here too," Guyman said. "It's not going to travel on Two Bar land."

"The bank's too steep," O'Malley argued, glancing apprehensively up toward Mary. It was not the bank he was worried about.

"There's a place ahead where it can come down. See that it does."

Guyman split his men, half riding on one side of the river, half on the other, back from the unpleasant drift of sheep dust. When they reached the spot where the bank flattened out, O'Malley rode up and helped Mary bring the wagon down. She did not ask him any questions, except with her eyes. The whole thing had been obvious enough.

Once a ewe pulled away from the band and headed up the bank, her lamb following. O'Malley touched spurs to his horse, but the ewe reached the top before he could stop her.

Two shots roared, frightening the other sheep. O'Malley reined up in helpless anger, the sharp smell of gunpowder reaching him on the stifling hot breeze. Hodge Guyman made a dry, triumphant grin with no humor in it and calmly thumbed two new cartridges into the cylinder of his .44. Julio watched with tears in his brown eyes, for the sheep were like his children.

The riders stayed until almost dark. They stood by silently while Julio and O'Malley brought the strung-out sheep together to bed them down.

Guyman's eyes lingered on Mary. "We're going home now, but we'll be back bright and early in the morning. You keep that coffee hot."

Not until after supper did Mary ask O'Malley, "Why did we get into a fix like this?"

He told her how long it would have taken had they turned back and headed south from San Angelo.

"But this way you might lose all the sheep," she argued.

"It's better to lose the sheep than to lose you."

Her mouth dropped open. Her eyes were wounded. For a moment she stared at him in hurt silence. "Did you think I would be leaving you, Larkin?"

He stared morosely into the campfire, poking aimlessly at the coals with a burned-off mesquite stick. "I couldn't have blamed you. You're a town girl, like your father said. This life is hard enough on men sometimes, but for a girl, a girl from town . . ."

His voice trailed off. He looked up and saw her temper change from deep hurt to a proud anger. "Why did you marry me then, Larkin, if you had so little faith in me?"

She arose stiffly and turned away from him. Pleading, he followed after her, but she would not listen to him. For a long time, then, he sat brooding at the dying campfire, watching the flashes of lightning that built in the west. He watched them, but he did not really see them at all.

Next morning the wind came out of the west, bringing patchy lead-gray clouds hurrying low overhead. The west wind was damp and cool, foretelling of rain somewhere. O'Malley's pulse quickened at the thought of rain. But there was an irony to it that did not escape him. Had it come a week earlier, he could have skirted around the Two Bar country. Now he was in the middle of it, and no amount of rain could change that.

Hodge Guyman arrived early. Arrogantly he rode into the middle of camp, heedless of the dust kicked up by his skittish, ear-twitching dun. It was a nervous young bronc with a hackamore over its head instead of a bridle and bit. That would be Guyman's way of making a show. And O'Malley knew who the show was for.

Guyman stepped down, took a tin cup without asking, and poured himself some black coffee. He did not have his crew with him, just Newt. Newt stopped outside of camp and led his horse in, as an old-time cowboy of good manners would do. He tipped his hat to Mary.

Guyman eased up to O'Malley's horse. Before O'Malley could move to stop him, he slipped the saddle gun out of its scabbard. He smashed the stock against an iron wagon rim and pitched the rifle into the wagon. Grinning, he stationed himself beside the wagon, where Mary had to pass close as she loaded the camp gear.

O'Malley clenched his fists, knowing he had to put up with it or see his flock wiped out. But he knew he could not put up with it long, sheep or no sheep. He gave Julio a signal, and they started the flock moving.

To the west the gray clouds darkened almost to black. The wind, so hot yesterday, now was cool with the stirring smell of rain that a drouth-hardened Texan can truly appreciate. Somewhere ahead, O'Malley thought, it must be raining torrents.

They had not been on the move long before a ewe up near the lead decided to take off on a cow trail that led up the bank. Seeing her, Julio Ramirez trotted heavily over to head her off.

Guyman was riding far back, near Mary and the wagon. Seeing Julio and the ewe, he jabbed spurs into the dun bronc. It made a couple of pitching jumps, but Guyman held its head up. Another time, maybe, he would let the bronc pitch its damnedest and put on a show. Right now he was more interested in beating the Mexican to that ewe.

But Julio had a head start. He was up on the bank first, waving his arms and shouting. The ewe wheeled and skittered back down to the flock. Guyman came charging up too late, his pistol out. In frustration he reined the bronc straight toward Julio.

The old Mexican tried to dodge, and the dun horse tried to miss him. But Guyman firmly jerked on the reins and slammed his mount into the herder. The impact flung Julio over the edge. He rolled down the steep incline.

Loping fearfully to him, seeing how crookedly the old Mexican lay there, O'Malley thought surely he would have some broken bones. For a moment his eyes stabbed at Guyman. He had to force down a wild urge to drag the man out of the saddle. But he had to take care of Julio. While he was doing that, Guyman rode away.

The old rider Newt came up and peered down the bank, shame in his eyes. "Your man hurt?"

The breath had been knocked out of Julio. When he tried to stand, he winced at the pain of it.

O'Malley said, "You'll do no more walking. You'll have to use the wagon."

Newt watched without comment as Mary brought the wagon. With Julio riding the wagon and O'Malley taking Julio's place afoot at the head of the band, it would be Mary's job to take O'Malley's horse and follow behind, keeping the drags moving. She accepted without saying anything. Her eyes were still angry. She did not look at O'Malley.

She retreated beneath the wagon's canvas cover and came out moments later wearing a pair of O'Malley's rolled-up trousers belted tightly around her slim waist. She swung onto the horse without accepting a foot lift. Her small boots, with Mexican spurs jingling on the heels, were far short of the stirrups when she sat in the saddle.

Looking back often from his place in front of the slow-moving flock, O'Malley could see her riding back there, and Julio bringing up the wagon. His face twisted in worry as he saw Hodge Guyman riding beside Mary, following her like a persistent dog when she tried to pull away.

The rain started, gentle at first but gradually beating heavier. The tiny pencil-thin stream slowly widened, its trickle of clear water turning chocolate with mud. As the water deepened, O'Malley could see that soon it would be impossible for his sheep to cross it. He began working back afoot, shoving all of them to the north side. Before long the stream was ten feet wide and moving rapidly.

O'Malley knew he could wait no longer. He led the sheep up the slanting riverbank, out and away from the water.

Guyman wasted no time in getting there. "What do you think you're doing?"

"This river's fixing to flood. I have to get these sheep up on the bank or they'll drown."

Hodge Guyman wore that grin again, cold as ice in January. "This up here is the Two Bar. That down yonder is the state property. You get back on it!"

He drew his pistol and sat there with it in his hand, looking like a coyote that had just caught a lamb. O'Malley took an angry step toward him, ready to force a showdown. The pistol lifted. O'Malley's mouth went thin with the fury that welled up in him.

"You can't afford to shoot me, Guyman."

"Maybe not, but I can shoot your sheep."

The gun barked twice, sending the sheep scurrying back down the bank, toward the water. All but two that would never go anywhere again.

O'Malley turned away, defeated. He could drag Guyman down and whip him up one side of the riverbank and down the other. He knew he was man enough to do it. But in the end Guyman would still be the winner. It would take two days at best before O'Malley could get his flock off of the Two Bar land. Guyman could bring his men and kill every sheep long before then.

All O'Malley could do now was to let the sheep string out as high up the bank as possible, hoping the water would not rise enough to sweep them away. One thing he knew —if he lost his sheep, he would take their price out of Guyman's hide. He would make Guyman eat that six-shooter, piece by piece.

The sheep edged ever higher as the water lapped up near their thin cloven hoofs. Once O'Malley looked back to see a big lamb slip down the muddy bank and tumble into the brown water, floundering helplessly until its heavy wool dragged it under.

Julio had taken the wagon up above, and Guyman had not tried to restrain him. Guyman was too busy. He was riding beside Mary, telling her all she might do, all she might have, if she would go with him. He reached across and touched her arm, and this time she did not pull away.

O'Malley stopped suddenly, his mouth open, the hot, jealous anger rising to his face.

He heard the faint rumbling noise somewhere upriver, obscured in the heavy beat of rain on the muddy ground, the rolling of water close to him. He sensed that a wall of it was coming down from somewhere ahead. But at the moment he cared mostly about Mary.

A black fury in him, O'Malley started back in a stiff trot, his fists knotted. Then he saw why Mary was letting Guyman ride up beside her, stirrup to stirrup.

Mary turned her foot outward, ever so little, and raked

her big Chihuahua spur rowel down the bronc's sensitive flank. The dun went straight up as if he had a fire in his tail. Caught by surprise, Guyman grabbed desperately at the saddle horn and managed somehow to catch hold of it. But his left stirrup was flopping free.

The bronc jumped again, sideways this time, as Mary sailed her wet hat under its nose. The right stirrup was flopping now. Guyman was up one side and down the other, helpless. The .44 sailed out of his holster and landed with a splash in the foaming water.

For one brief moment it looked as if Guyman would hang onto the saddle. Then he went down, his eyes and mouth wide open, into the dirty, churning water. The bronc pitched across the river and up the far bank, headed for home. Mary spurred along behind it, shouting, keeping it on the run.

Guyman pulled to his feet, swaying, coughing, the water swirling around his hips. He demanded that Newt catch his horse.

Newt eased through the rising water, in no hurry. Smiling, he looked back over his shoulder. "I'll try to catch him, Hodge. Don't you go away." He set off in a slow trot, taking his time.

Still boiling mad, O'Malley waded after Guyman, swinging his fists. Guyman was strong, and he was mean. But he had a bellyful of dirty water, and O'Malley had the wild strength that comes from an Irish rage. Guyman never had a chance.

The third time O'Malley dragged Guyman up out of the mud and water to pound him some more, Mary pushed her horse between them. "There's a big rise of water coming yonder. Even the sheep have got sense enough to get up out of the way."

O'Malley had to half carry Guyman up the north side because the man had so little strength left in him. Before long the river was bank full. Heavy clouds to the west promised to keep it that way. Guyman did not look like the colonel's son now. Afoot, his hat gone, his muddy clothes clinging to him, his lips blue with cold, he looked like a half-drowned banty rooster.

"It may be a couple of days before you can get back across," O'Malley told him. "Even if your friends come to help you, they can't do much from the other side. And maybe by then we'll be off of the Two Bar country for good."

There wasn't any fight left in Guyman now. "Two days is a long time to go without grub. You ain't going to pull out and leave me here to starve, are you?"

A malicious gleam came to O'Malley's eyes, and he began to smile for the first time in days. "We're not leaving anything here for you. But if you want to come along and help us drive the sheep, we'll see that you eat."

O'Malley thought Guyman was going to die right there in front of him. He shrugged. "Suit yourself," he said, and turned away.

But when he looked back later he saw Guyman trudging along in muddy boots, shoving wool-soaked sheep before him.

O'Malley walked slowly beside his wife, trying hard to think of the right thing to say. All that came was, "Forgive me, Mary."

She smiled the smile that had drawn him to her the first time he had seen her in San Antonio. "That I will, Larkin O'Malley. But remember this—I have the blood of Michael Donovan in my veins, and there's no quitting in the Donovans. Many a time I've seen my father mad and disgusted almost to busting, the way I was. And then he would go on and do a better job than he'd ever done before.

"You've seen me mad, and I've no doubt you'll see me mad again. But it doesn't mean I'm quitting you, Larkin. It just means you'll have to get a move on you if you want to keep up with me."

Smiling, Larkin O'Malley squeezed her hand and pulled her down from the horse to kiss her. Then he looked toward his sheep, strung out atop the riverbank, and he got a move on.

KELTON
ON
KELTON

I was born at a place called Horse Camp on the Scharbauer Cattle Company's Five Wells Ranch in Andrews County, Texas, in 1926. My father was a cowboy there, and my grandfather was the ranch foreman. My great-grandfather had come out from East Texas about 1876 with a wagon and a string of horses to become a ranchman, but he died young, leaving four small boys to grow up as cowpunchers and bronc breakers. With all that heritage I should have become a good cowboy myself, but somehow I never did, so I decided if I could not do it I would write about it.

I studied journalism at the University of Texas and became a livestock and farm reporter in San Angelo, Texas, writing fiction as a sideline to newspaper work. I have maintained the two careers in parallel more than thirty years. My fiction has been mostly about Texas, about areas whose history and people I know from long study and long personal acquaintance. I have always believed we can learn much about ourselves by studying our history, for we are the products of all that has gone before us. All history is relevant today, because the way we live—the values we believe in—are a result of molds prepared for us by our forebears a long time ago.

I was an infantryman in World War II and married an Austrian girl, Anna, I met there shortly after the war. We raised three children, all grown now and independent, proud of their mixed heritage of the Old World on one hand and the Texas frontier on the other.

BANTAM'S #1
ALL-TIME BESTSELLING AUTHOR
AMERICA'S FAVORITE FRONTIER WRITER

☐	25398	THE LONESOME GODS	$3.95
☐	24133	LAW OF THE DESERT BORN	$2.95
☐	25328	TO TAME A LAND	$2.95
☐	23132	SHADOW RIDERS	$2.95
☐	26176	COMSTOCK LODE	$3.95
☐	26039	YONDERING	$2.95
☐	24763	MILO TALON	$2.95
☐	25200	THE STRONG SHALL LIVE	$2.95
☐	26446	BENDIGO SHAFTER	$3.95
☐	25098	THE KEY-LOCK MAN	$2.95
☐	24922	RADIGAN	$2.95
☐	23258	WAR PARTY	$2.50
☐	24905	KIOWA TRAIL	$2.95
☐	24912	THE BURNING HILLS	$2.95
☐	24858	SHALAKO	$2.95
☐	24867	KILRONE	$2.95
☐	25771	THE RIDER OF LOST CREEK	$2.95
☐	24759	CALLAGHEN	$2.95
☐	25478	THE QUICK AND THE DEAD	$2.95
☐	20795	OVER ON THE DRY SIDE	$2.50
☐	24904	DOWN THE LONG HILLS	$2.95
☐	24766	WESTWARD THE TIDE	$2.95
☐	24748	KID RODELO	$2.95
☐	24847	BROKEN GUN	$2.95
☐	25195	WHERE THE LONG GRASS BLOWS	$2.95
☐	24780	HOW THE WEST WAS WON	$2.95

Prices and availability subject to change without notice.

Short Story Collections from
LOUIS L'AMOUR

"Bantam Books is the only publisher authorized to issue my short stories in book form."

—*Louis L'Amour.*

☐	26393	**THE RIDER OF THE RUBY HILLS**	$2.95
☐	26392	**THE TRAIL TO CRAZY MAN**	$2.95
☐	26189	**RIDING FOR THE BRAND**	$2.95
☐	26188	**DUTCHMAN'S FLAT**	$2.95
☐	23368	**BOWDRIE**	$2.95
☐	24550	**BOWDRIE'S LAW**	$2.95
☐	24764	**BUCKSKIN RUN**	$2.95
☐	24134	**THE HILLS OF HOMICIDE**	$2.95
☐	24133	**LAW OF THE DESERT BORN**	$2.95
☐	25200	**THE STRONG SHALL LIVE**	$2.95
☐	25393	**WAR PARTY**	$2.95
☐	26039	**YONDERING**	$2.95

Look for them at your bookstore or use this coupon for ordering: